Big Sandy

Big Sandy
Stories

Marsha Walker

OPENEYE PRESS 2016
DENVER, COLORADO

Big Sandy, Stories by Marsha Walker
Print edition ISBN: 978-0-692-71568-0
Copyright © 2016 by Marsha Walker
All rights reserved. No part of this publication may be reproduced or transmitted in any form or by any means, electronic or mechanical, including photo-copying, recording or by any information storage and retrieval system, without permission. Reviewers may quote brief passages.

Book Format and Cover by AE Books Denver, CO
Published by OPENEYE PRESS 2016

for my parents

Table of Contents

Hall's Court, 1971 ... p3

Billy ... p17

The Bulgarian ... p29

Super Freak ... p65

Sharon Smith ... p81

Roswell, New Mexico ... p95

The Adjunct ... p109

Big Sandy ... p129

Big Sandy

Hall's Court, 1971

Old Nanny Hall marched out to third base where Amy crouched like a cat, trying to steal home.

Jen rolled the ball. Little Charlie, who was Nanny's grandson, ran up to it and kicked it hard. The ball flew out to left field. It would have been a home run if a car hadn't been parked there. The ball bounced off the car and chubby Ellen, who already had breasts and wore deodorant, caught it. "You're out," she screamed. The other team was up. Nanny stood behind Amy now. In spite of her emphysema, Nanny took the last puff off a cigarette and tossed the smoldering butt on the ground and stamped it out.

"I need to talk to you, sissy," Nanny pleaded.

What could old Nanny Hall want with her, Amy wondered.

Nanny put her arm around Amy's shoulder and ushered her off the playing field, the parking lot of the eight-unit apartment complex that Nanny owned. A dozen kids from the neighborhood stopped to watch and to complain.

"Where are you taking her?" they yelled. "She's our catcher!"

"She'll be back in a minute," Nanny yelled back. "Play on!"

Nanny guided Amy to the front porch of her split-level ranch home, which sat amongst the apartment building and several other homes the Halls had built and sold in the cul-de-sac named for the Hall family. Nanny lived with her husband J.D. and various children, grandchildren and great-grandchildren who came and went. Downtown there was Hall's Furniture, a car dealership and a bowling alley called Hall's Paradise Lanes. Amy's mother said the Halls were rich, and that Nanny and her daughters were the ones who ran things since J.D. had a heart attack a few years back. Nanny opened the front door and motioned for Amy to go inside.

"Here now, sis, let's go in and talk a minute."

Amy followed Nanny up a small set of stairs and stood in the middle of the freezing cold living room while Nanny disappeared in the kitchen. Framed photographs of Nanny's large family covered the walls. Nanny emerged from the kitchen with a tall glass of soda for herself and nothing for Amy.

"Sit down there, sis, on the divan."

Amy sat and stared at the coffee table. On one end were several large photo albums stacked neatly on a white crocheted doily like her great-grandmother made and gave to everyone at Christmas. On the other, ceramic figurines of maidens and elves were staged as if in conversation. A full dirty ashtray sat on top of *The Holy Bible*. Nanny sat down heavily across from Amy in a blue recliner, the only piece of furniture not covered in plastic.

Hall's Court, 1971

"Now, sis," Nanny said gravely, looking Amy right in the eye. "I'm going to ask you a question and I want you to tell me the absolute truth."

Amy nodded. Her heart was pounding now.

"I want to know how that big hole got in your living room wall."

Amy looked down at her worn tennis shoes. She felt Nanny's eyes on her. Except for the roar of an air conditioner the house was still. "I don't know."

"You don't know? Well, think real hard for a minute."

Amy pretended to think hard. She looked upward and sighed. "Wasn't it there when we moved in?" she offered feebly.

"No, it certainly was not," Nanny protested. "It sure was not, sis. No sir. I have my apartments overhauled every time somebody moves in or out." Nanny leaned forward. "Now, sis, I know you don't want to get nobody in trouble, but I need to know how that hole got there." While she waited for Amy to respond, she took a cigarette out of a leather case and reached down inside her shirt and bra, fumbling around for several uncomfortable seconds as Amy watched until, finally, her hand emerged with a silver lighter. She lit the cigarette, took a draw and exhaled loudly. "Is that what that ruckus was about the other night?"

"What ruckus?" Amy asked, as if she didn't know.

"Now sis, your mommy had the police up to your place at three o'clock in the morning the other night. Like to woke the whole neighborhood up."

"I think it was there before the ruckus," Amy said, feeling cornered now. "Yeah, it was."

Heavy blue drapes framed a large window. The kickball game went on. Amy could hear the other kids shouting, "Run!"

"Was it your daddy who made the hole in the wall?"

"I don't know. Why don't you ask him?" She knew this was a smart-aleck answer.

"Well, he don't come around 'til the middle of the night usually. That's why I don't ask him!"

Amy's face burned with embarrassment.

"Were you awake when it happened?"

"No, I was asleep. When I came down the next morning it was like that already."

"That right?" Nanny sighed, realizing she had given the little girl a way out. Amy was the same age as her grandson, Little Charlie. They were both seven. The Pritchett family had been renting with Nanny since Amy was a baby. They started out in the old building, in a one-bedroom attic apartment. Billy was still driving a cab then. Once he got on at the coke plant they moved to a basement unit with the two small bedrooms. Nanny recalled replacing a windowpane someone had knocked out in that one. Just before Barb and Billy split up for the last time, they moved into the new building of two-bedroom townhomes. Those apartments had plush, shag carpeting and central air. Barb worked at a hotel restaurant across the river in Huntington, West Virginia. She drove back and forth two times a day to do the lunch and dinner shifts. She was never late with the rent.

"I woke up and it was just like that is all I know," Amy said.

"Uh," Nanny grunted.

"Can I go now?"

"You sure you don't know nothin' about that hole?"

Amy shook her head. "Nope. Can I go?"

"I reckon, if you're really tellin' the truth." Nanny leaned across the coffee table and put her face so close to Amy's she could see the lines on the old woman's bifocals. "Now, are you sis? Are you tellin' the whole truth? You know Jesus don't like fibbers."

"That's the truth as far as I know." Then Amy tore down the stairs and out the front door, grateful to feel the hot, humid air again. She rejoined the kickball game. They played until dark, when parents called their children in for the night. Amy told her mother what happened. "Nanny was asking about the hole in the wall."

"What! How did she know about it?" Her mother was still wearing her hotel restaurant uniform. "Lord," her mother said, throwing up her hands. "She'll be calling me or over here one. You can count on that. She won't let nothing rest. Once she gets her teeth into something she's like an old bulldog."

The next morning Nanny Hall knocked on the front door. Amy's grandmother was babysitting.

"Mae, I want to have a look at that hole in the wall," Nanny said. "If you don't mind, honey."

Her grandmother opened the screen door and let Nanny in. From the doorway Nanny quickly surveyed the living room and the stairway, inspecting the carpet and the walls. Amy and Maryanne were watching *Captain Kangaroo*.

"There it is. Well, I'll be," Nanny said, shaking her head at the sight of it. Nanny carried a small notebook and a wooden ruler. She stood in front of the hole with her hands on her hips, staring at it. "I just had this paint done not a year ago." Nanny held the ruler over the hole and measured. Amy's father had been aiming for the television, but he missed because he was drunk, putting his foot through the wall instead. Amy and Maryanne watched the whole thing from the top of the stairs. "Five or six inches across," she said.

Amy's grandmother stood in the doorway with her arms crossed, wearing her usual floral housedress and slippers. "Sounds about right," she agreed.

"Now, Mae, you and I both know who did this," Nanny said. "You don't have to defend him."

"Oh, I won't defend him," her grandmother said.

"I just need someone to say he did it. I'm going to make him pay for this," Nanny griped. "What was he doing over here at three o'clock in the morning in the first place? I thought he and Barb split up for good."

"Barb wants a divorce," her grandmother said. "He was mad."

"Good for her," Nanny said. "Good for her. I'm about fed up with drunks myself."

Hall's Court, 1971

Nanny paused for a few breaths, gathering energy for a tirade. "You wouldn't believe what I put up with over here, Mae," she started in. "The police is over here once a week on somebody. You know that couple over in Unit 3? Why, couple weeks ago he liked to choke that girl to death! They had to take her to the hospital and she still has bruises around her neck. They tore the railing off the stairs fightin' and carryin' on."

Her grandmother shook her head and offered her standard comment for just about everything: "Well."

Nanny fanned herself with her small writing pad. "Mae, the money I collect in rent I turn right around into maintenance and repairs. There's hardly no profit in it."

"That right," her grandmother offered, more to confirm than to ask. "Well."

"Oh, honey, no. On top of that, I got to put up with all these shenanigans," Nanny said, nodding at the ugly hole. "I got to chase after people to pay rent. I'm a-tellin' you what, I'd like to get out of the landlord business." The way Nanny was carrying on, Amy thought the old woman might cry. "You got a pot of soup beans on the stove, don't you, honey? They sure smell good!"

Her grandmother asked Nanny if she would like to sit down.

"No thanks, Mae. I got to keep moving." She adjusted her bra straps with a snap. "I got so much to do today. If I sit down I might not get back up. How you been, honey?"

"I'm still here," her grandmother said.

"You've got that arthritis too, don't you? Where is it now? In your feet?"

"Oh, Lord, yes," her grandmother said.

"I've got it in both my hips now. I can't hardly walk."

"Well."

"Mae, you know I've never had a problem with Barb paying her rent on time, bless her heart. Not one time in all these years she's rented from me has she been late with the rent. I know it's not been easy with everything she's been through," Nanny said, looking over at the girls, "with all that's on her shoulders now. I hate to come over here and trouble her with this. Barb's a good woman, hardworking too. It just don't figure—her and Billy Pritchett. I never have understood how in the world she got mixed up with the likes of him."

On close examination, Amy decided that her mother was right. Nanny was like an old bulldog. She was jowly and short and stumpy. When she talked to you, she set her eyes on to yours like she was homing in on a target. Nanny leaned in toward Amy's grandmother as if they were sharing a secret.

"My daughter, Jean, she's in the same boat. Big Charlie ain't worth a dime neither. He's not mean but he's do-less and half drunk most of the day. He works down at the steel mill, but Jean, bless her heart, she's got to do everything around the house, plus helping me. He won't even mow the lawn!" Nanny paused for a minute to take a few breaths. When she spoke again, her voice was low, almost a whisper.

Hall's Court, 1971

"You know I grew up with some of Billy's people out on Bear Creek, don't you? Billy had an aunt who married one of my cousins. Naomi was her name. Naomi was the sweetest person you ever met, but the rest of that Pritchett clan," Nanny lowered her voice even more. "Why some of them Pritchetts been in the penitentiary even!"

"They were a rough bunch," her grandmother agreed.

"I'm not tellin' you nothin' you don't already know, am I?" Nanny asked in a normal voice again, waving her hand dismissively. "But it just breaks my heart. Nice woman like Barb, having to struggle so. It's a shame is what it is."

Captain Kangaroo was talking to Mr. Green Jeans.

"Well, Mae, I'm sorry to disturb you, honey," Nanny said. "You better tend to those beans now." Nanny made her way to the door. "Tell Barb I'll send one of my grandsons over here to fix that hole in a couple days."

"Will do," her grandmother said.

"Sit down now and get off your feet, Mae," Nanny ordered. "Talk to you later."

Last year Nanny installed a small in-ground swimming pool to the side of her house that she allowed her tenants to use. During the day she supervised things as she came and went from her chores. She wore a white hat and clip-on sunglasses and baggy shorts. When she went in for lunch everyone had to leave. Amy and some neighborhood kids were playing Harriet the Spy. Amy was Harriet. Little Charlie, and Tommy from one street over were helping her spy. They hid behind a car, in their damp swimsuits, and watched the parking lot, looking for suspicious behavior. Bored, Tommy and Joe went home to eat lunch. Amy and Charlie gave up on spying and walked through a small patch of woods to the elementary school's deserted playground. They were climbing on the monkey bars when Charlie said, "Your daddy kicked a hole in your living room wall, didn't he?"

"Yeah," Amy said. She was hanging upside down. She flipped herself over and landed perfectly on her feet. "He was drunk."

Charlie had short blonde hair, cut military style close to his head like his grandfather's. His front teeth stuck out and he was scrawny.

"I have to go in," Charlie said.

"Why?"

"I gotta poop," he said. "Bad."

They started back towards the apartment complex. They were almost through the woods when Amy had a brilliant idea.

"Why don't you poop outside?"

"What?"

"Do it outside."

Charlie smiled devilishly. "Where? In the woods?"

"No," Amy said. "I think you should do it on Nanny's back porch. Make her think some old dog did it."

Charlie agreed immediately, delighted to set forth on a project of mischief. They ran the rest of the way through the woods to Nanny's house. Charlie went inside to make sure his grandmother was out of sight while Amy waited on the back porch.

Hall's Court, 1971

"Coast is clear! She's watching *Days of Our Lives*," he whispered loudly. His eyes were big with excitement.

"Hurry!" Amy said.

There were no trees or bushes to hide behind. The porch was a cement platform with two reclining lawn chairs and two clay pots of red and white petunias sitting at either corner. Only a few small trees that lined the chain link fence separated Nanny's house from an alley.

"You do it too!" Charlie said. "If I get caught she'll beat the tar out of me."

"I don't have to go number two."

"Then just pee."

"Okay," she agreed.

"On three," he said.

"One, two, three!"

They pulled down their pants and stuck their butts out. It took a minute for any pee to come. Amy watched a yellow stream form around her feet. They kept their eyes on the sliding glass doors, making sure Nanny didn't pass by.

"I'm done." Amy pulled up her red velvet bikini bottoms. Pee dripped down her legs. Charlie was straining, but then two turds dropped on the porch.

"Let's go!"

They fell on each other as they ran from the scene of the crime. When they got to the front yard, they slowed down and tried to act normal. Nanny was standing on the front porch, shaking out a rug.

"What are you two up to?"

"Nothing," Charlie said, grinning. "Can we go back in the pool now?"

"Fifteen more minutes," Nanny said. "Go in and eat something, Charlie."

"I'm not hungry."

"Go on in and eat anyway," she ordered, pointing at the front door. "You can't run around on an empty stomach, son!"

Charlie hung his head and ran towards the house. Amy walked to the pool. Neighbors were gathering at the entrance, waiting for Nanny to unlock the gate. Carol Anne, whose husband, Bob, had tried to choke her not long ago, stood with her two young sons, holding towels and a float. Carol Anne wore cutoff shorts and a halter top. Amy couldn't see any bruises on her neck now, but she had watched from her bedroom window the night the police came and made Bob sit in the squad car. Other neighbors sat on coolers, talking or listening to portable radios. Finally, Nanny appeared in her white hat, shaking the big ring of keys she carried around all day like a tambourine. She unlocked the gate and went back inside her house. Amy headed over to Nanny's back porch. The turds were still there. There was just a damp spot now where Amy had peed. She ran to the other end of the yard behind a tree. She picked up a small rock and threw it at the sliding glass door, but nobody came. She threw a couple more. After a while, Charlie appeared at the door.

"She went to the A&P," he said.

Hall's Court, 1971

They looked down at the still moist turds.

"Let's go swim," he said.

They played in the pool into the afternoon, when Nanny left to fix dinner and Charlie's mother, Jean, took over the watch.

Amy and Charlie followed Nanny to her house, giggling and whispering behind her. Charlie's mess was still there.

"I have to go again!" he said. Charlie struggled to get his wet swimsuit down. Then he squatted, shamelessly, next to the garbage can while Amy kept an eye out. Charlie left two more turds in front of the sliding glass doors. Then they ran in the direction of the street. Amy kept running.

The next morning the two piles were still there. Charlie added one more. Amy peed again.

"Wonder why she don't come out and look at 'em?" he asked sadly. Amy and Charlie stood there looking at the turds, as if they were orphans nobody wanted or paid any attention to.

"Don't know," Amy said. "Knock on the door and run."

Charlie went to the glass door and pounded hard with his fist. They ran. Nanny was coming in the other direction, holding a switch. She had an awful look on her face.

"Charlie!" she growled. "Get over here right now, son!"

Charlie tried to run by her, but Nanny grabbed his arm.

"Come here to me!" she yelled. "And you! You get on home, you nasty little girl!" Nanny pointed and squinted at her. "Your mother over there working herself to the bone for you and you over here pullin' this stunt! You really showed yourself today, girl! Nasty! Just plain nasty!"

Charlie strained against Nanny's grip. He started whining pathetically. Amy felt sorry for him.

"Hush now, son!" Nanny looked back at Amy who hadn't moved. "Get on home now before I light in on you too. I'm so mad now it's hard tellin' what I might do!"

Nanny turned her attention back to Charlie. "Stand still!" Amy took off running. Nanny lit into Charlie with the switch. Neighbors came out of their houses and apartments to see what the fuss was about. Nanny switched Charlie all the way to the front door as he screamed and cried. Amy hid behind the apartment building and listened until they went inside.

Billy

"Boogie doo! Boogie doo!"

That's what her father said when he teased her. It was nonsense language and her mother didn't like it. She thought it sounded vulgar.

"Billy, stop it!" her mother huffed. "Don't you know anything about talking to kids?"

For a change Billy had come to visit when he was sober. The coke plant where he worked had been on strike for weeks, but he said he would take everyone out for a steak dinner if her mother did his laundry. He was sprawled on the couch watching a John Wayne movie on the television.

"What's the matter? Your girlfriend not around this weekend?"

"Barb, don't start up."

Her mother was pushing a mop around the kitchen floor angrily. Amy grabbed Billy's sock and tried to pull it off.

"Boogie doo!" he said. He yanked his foot away. "Get your daddy a Pepsi with some ice in it, would you? I'm gonna take y'all out for dinner as soon as this movie is over," Billy boasted. "Get ready."

"I thought you were so hard up," her mom said. "Where did you get money for a steak dinner?"

"Barb?" her father said, pausing for effect, "must you debate every issue?" A piece of stuffing from the hole in the couch fell on him. He gingerly picked it off his shirt and stuffed it back inside the hole. "Billy Pritchett has always got enough money to take his girls out for dinner."

At the steakhouse Billy said, "Get whatever you want."

So they did. They moved down the buffet with their trays, taking baked potatoes, mashed potatoes, French fries, green beans, pecan pie, Jello and soft drinks. Amy ordered a T-bone steak. Her mother ordered the filet mignon, and for Maryanne her mother chose an expensive ribeye she knew would go to waste. Behind the counter, men with sweaty faces cooked the meat on a flaming grill. They walked with their loaded trays and sat on benches around a rustic-looking table, her mother and father on one side and Maryanne and Amy on the other. A stuffed deer's head hung over them, its dull lifeless eyes fixed straight ahead. A waitress wearing a short brown skirt and cowboy hat brought their sizzling steaks to the table.

"Your Aunt Naomi give you some money?" her mother asked. "Or you been gambling?"

"Barb, do we have to go into that now?" Billy asked. "You're like a broken record, just skipping over the same line. He mimicked her in a falsetto voice: "Your aunt give you some money? Where'd you get the money, Billy? Naomi give you some money? Where'd you get the money, Billy?" He stopped to laugh. "I don't have any money, Billy. When you gonna give me some money, Billy?" Barb listened, stone-faced. To look at them from across the room, Amy thought, they looked like any other family at the restaurant.

Her parents' bickering continued through dinner and into the evening after they returned home until Billy fell asleep on the couch. The girls were watching *Walt Disney*. "Billy, go home," her mother ordered.

"I am home," he said with closed eyes.

"Like hell you are," her mother snapped. "Now go on. I've gotta get up early tomorrow morning and I don't want to fool with you."

"Damn woman!" he griped. "I bought this couch!"

"And I'm still paying for it!" her mother yelled. "Now get your laundry and go on!"

A week later the child support check came in the mail. Her mother threw the envelope on the floor and paced around it, cursing and stomping on it. "Son of a bitch," she said over and over. She was wearing her hotel lounge uniform: velvet hot pants and a matching vest with dark stockings and black, fake-leather boots. It was late. The girls were already in their pajamas. Amy was reading *Harriet the Spy* again. Maryanne was upstairs. "Get your coats on!" her mother commanded.

Amy and Maryanne dressed quickly. Her mother drove down I-23, along the railroad tracks that ran next to the coke plant where her father worked. Flames shot out of the smokestacks, brightening the night sky. You could see the fires burning in the ovens. There was no sign of his car at the motel where he had been renting a room since Billy and Barb separated, and it wasn't at his girlfriend's house either.

"What did he do this time?" Amy asked.

Her mother crossed the Ohio River Bridge and headed over to Ironton.

"He docked us for the steak dinners."

The night streets of Ironton, Ohio, were dead. Even in broad daylight, it wasn't much of a place since the factory shut down. Now people only came here to buy alcohol since you couldn't buy it legally in Big Sandy, Kentucky, because it was dry. Her mother pulled up in front of a bar. A sign above the entrance said: The Sugar Shack. Amy could hear loud music.

"See his car?"

Amy craned her neck to look. Normal-looking houses lined the streets. Two men walked towards the bar, laughing.

"I don't see it," her mother said. "Do you?"

They watched people come and go from the bar for a while until her mother said, "I'm tired. Let's go home."

The next morning they went back to the motel. His car still wasn't there. Her mother checked at the front desk. The tiny office smelled of cigar smoke.

"He done moved," the old man behind the desk said. "He got a place with a buddy is what he told me."

"Where?" her mother demanded.

"Ridge Road is all he said, but they ain't but a few houses up there. That's all I know about it."

They got back in the car and raced through town, out towards the county. Just beyond the Foodland they turned off the main highway and drove up a steep hill. Her mother slowed to examine each house carefully. There were a couple of A-frames and a few fancier ranch homes. None looked like the type of place her father would live.

"I don't see his car," her mother said.

Further down the road, there was a split-level ranch home set back in the trees away from the road. Several cars were parked in front, including her father's LTD. Her mother pulled in the long driveway. "What the hell is going on?" she said to herself. The house was big but it wasn't kept up like the others. There were no potted flowers on the porch, and the grass in the huge front yard needed mowing. The paint on the second floor was peeling.

"Let's just go," Amy suggested, nervous now.

"Stay in the car," her mother said. "It's no tellin' who or what he's got in there."

Her mother knocked on the front door several times before a man wearing only blue jeans appeared. She spoke to the man briefly and they disappeared behind the door. Amy examined the house carefully. It was late morning. Dense woods surrounded the house on three sides. The exterior of the first floor was made of gray stone, the second floor, of white clapboard. There was a two-car garage and a bay window. All the windows were bare. Cardboard boxes were strewn across the porch. She didn't recognize any of the other cars. From the driveway there was a pretty view of the rolling hills, thick with trees, whose leaves were turning gold and red. Amy listened as the wind blew through them. For a minute, she fantasized that this was her real house, freshly painted and kept up. She pictured nice furniture in the living room like she saw on television.

It seemed like her mother had been in the house for a long time when Amy and Maryanne decided to knock on the front door, which was ajar. Amy could hear voices inside. "Mommy?" The girls stood on a hardwood floor in a wide foyer, looking into an empty room with a large stone fireplace. The furniture consisted of lawn chairs and milk crates. There were empty bags of chips and paper plates on the floor. A stereo system sat on cardboard boxes. Albums and eight-track tapes were stacked beside it. Her father's old guitar lay in its case in the corner. Amy heard voices in another room and walked towards them. More trash and empty bottles of liquor and beer cans were piled in a garbage bag in a corner. In the kitchen the same man who answered the door and a blonde woman in a silky robe sat at a table. The man was wearing a shirt now.

"Where's our mom?" Amy asked loudly.

The man stood and walked passed them down a hallway.

"Hey, Billy? Your kids is down here!" he yelled up the stairway. "Y'all better get down here."

Amy stared at the blonde woman.

Billy

"Are y'all Barb's kids?" the woman asked. "Why, you're cute as buttons!" She had a raspy voice. "Roy," she said, "ain't these girls the cutest things you ever saw?" Amy noted that the woman sounded country, like her hillbilly relatives who used words like "ain't" and said "har" instead of hair.

"She's dressed them alike even," the woman kept on. "Look at'em! They're like little dollbabies. Roy, come in here and look at these dollbabies."

Roy stepped back in the kitchen. "They're cute." He lit a cigarette and rubbed his eyes. "My head is about to split in two."

"How old are you, girls?" the woman asked.

"I'm ten and she's seven," Amy said flatly. "Where's our mother?"

The woman's mascara was smeared under her eyes. Her hair was not really blonde. Her black roots were growing out and the more Amy looked at the woman the older she seemed to become. There was a large bottle of vodka and a can of tomato juice on the table. Her mother and Billy came down the stairway and shuffled towards the kitchen. "I wish I had cute little girls like you," the blonde lady said. "I'd give anything."

Her mother had been crying. Billy was wearing jeans and a shiny blue shirt that wasn't buttoned right. "Girls, you go on back to the car," her mother said as she wiped her eyes. "I don't want you exposed to this. Go on."

"Why are you crying? Did he hurt you?" Amy asked. She let go of Maryanne's hand and walked towards her mother.

"Not physically," her mother said, wiping more tears away. She held a roll of toilet paper in her hand. She unrolled a long piece and blew her nose loudly.

"Them's cute matching outfits, Barb," the blonde woman said, though nobody was paying her any attention now. "Where'd you get those?"

There were more female voices and noises coming from the top of the stairs. The grown-ups looked at each other—the blonde woman whose name was Sue Anne; Roy, who worked at the coke plant with her father; and her parents, Billy and Barb. The women on the stairs seemed to be grumbling about something. When they finally appeared in the kitchen, Amy identified one of them as Bunny Jones, her father's girlfriend. Her real name was Betty. She was tall with long blonde hair, big breasts and a pretty face. She was a teller at a bank. Amy had seen her once before, when her mother caught her father with Bunny at a bar in Ironton. Her mother had surprised them in the parking lot. That night Bunny wore a glittery dress. Her blonde hair was teased out, making her look taller than Billy. Today she wore a short robe that showed off her long legs, but her hair was flat and stringy. The other woman was a homely brunette with mangled teeth that she tried to hide with her hand when she spoke. Her name was Heather. She looked far younger than Bunny or the other blonde lady, who Amy figured now to be drunk by the way she was slumped in the chair and talking and laughing stupidly to herself. In fact, Heather didn't look much older than one of Amy's teenage babysitters. Heather stood in her bare feet, wearing an oversized pink Myrtle Beach t-shirt and cutoff shorts. Amy couldn't tell what was going on, what had happened, or why everyone was here in this strange house. Now that everyone was in the same room, no one seemed to know what to do next.

Bunny spoke with her hand on her hip. "Barb," she whined. "You and Billy is legally separated. Why do you care if he sees other women?"

"That's right, Barb," Roy said. "You kicked him out."

"After this thing broke up our marriage," her mother yelled, pointing at Bunny.

"You got no right to barge in like that," Heather ventured. Heather, too, sounded like one of her hillbilly cousins. "You got no right, lady."

"After today, I don't care who he sees," her mother said. "I never want to lay eyes on him again. I just didn't want my girls exposed to this kind of sordid thing."

Bunny said, "Well, you brought them out here."

"Yeah, lady," Heather chimed in.

"Hush your mouths," her mother warned, pointing a finger at them. "Leave my kids out of this. This is the sickest thing I've ever seen. Neither one of you is fit to be in the same room with my kids."

"You can't say a thing about what we do now," Bunny said.

"You can't say a thing about it, lady," Heather repeated.

"Heather," Billy said finally. "Just don't say anything, you ignoramus. Neither one of you Einsteins say another damn word."

Bunny reared up. "Billy Pritchett, let's get something straight right here and now," she ordered, pointing at him. "You don't talk to me like that." Billy waved his hand at Bunny as if to tune her out. Bunny turned and stomped up the stairs. "That's it," Bunny yelled from a few steps up, "I've had it with this situation!"

"Look what you done now," Heather said. She was sassing Billy, but she didn't look sure of herself. Her shoulders were hunched like she was about to get hit.

"Shut up," Billy said. Her father started towards Heather. Heather backed up a few inches

"Easy, Billy," Roy said. "That's my niece."

"You're both filth," her mother said, snarling and shaking her head with disgust. "Pure filth."

"I'll swear!" the old blonde lady said. She was laughing. "This is better than *Days of Our Lives!*"

Her mother grabbed Amy and Maryanne's hands. "Of all the lowdown stunts you've pulled on me, this one tops them all." She stomped dramatically towards the door, dragging Amy and Maryanne behind her. They went outside. Billy followed them.

"What happened?" Amy asked again.

"Nevermind! Just get in the car!"

Her father trailed after them and stood in the yard, swaying back and forth. Heather stuck her head out the door. They got in the car. Her mother was cursing. She put the car in reverse but instead of backing out of the driveway, she shifted gears again and aimed the car right at Billy and hit the gas. "Son of a bitch!" her mother yelled.

It took Billy a few seconds to register the car was coming right at him. Amy heard Heather scream, "Get out of the way!" Billy looked confused and suddenly terrified. He ran, stumbling and slipping pathetically on the wet grass. Her mother missed him by a few feet. Her mother's car was fully in the yard now. She shifted gears again, backed up and aimed the car at Billy. He ran in the other direction, dodging the car like a game of tag and fell into some bushes. Bunny appeared on the porch, fully clothed now, and started jumping up and down.

"Stop that crazy bitch!"

Roy came out of the house with a baseball bat and ran toward her mother's car. Her mother put the car in reverse and backed recklessly out of the driveway. They drove off at high speed, like criminals, back towards town. Amy saw Bunny and Heather run to help Billy out of the bushes. Then the strange house and the hysterical people running around the yard disappeared behind the trees.

The Bulgarian

For over a month now Amy sat behind the new guy in French class. His father was the new warden at the federal prison near her house in eastern Kentucky. William and his older, beautiful twin sisters had moved from Lompoc, California. The school was abuzz with the arrival of the three California transplants. Amy and William had never spoken, so this morning Amy was thrilled when William turned to face her and asked to borrow a pencil.

"*Je suis, tu es, il est,*" the students repeated after Madame Sparks. Amy leaned forward and inhaled the air around William's head. "*Repetez après moi, classe! Je vais, tu vas...*"

Madame Sparks, filled with enthusiasm from her recent trip to Paris, adjusted her silk scarf as she listened to the class' lethargic response.

"*Plus fort!*"

A month ago William stood at the front of the class with Madame Sparks. His tall, skinny body drooped listlessly over her stocky, soldier-like physique as she introduced him with his newly assigned

French name: *Guillaume*. She held his arm firmly, as if to prop him up or to prevent him from bolting out of the room.

"*Classe, je vous présente, Guillaume.*"

Everyone looked William over. Snickers from a couple of rednecks sitting in the back were squelched immediately by one stamp of Madame Sparks' foot. William smiled in a forced way that made him look like he might burst into tears at any second.

"*Répétez après moi: Bonjour, Guillaume!*"

"Bahn-jeerrr, Geee-yawwm!" the class dutifully repeated.

Madame Sparks guided William to his seat that alphabetically landed him in front of Amy's. When he sat down his desk made a loud squeaking noise, causing the class to turn and stare at him again. Because of his nice clothes and shy manner, some of the jocks and Vo-Tech guys called him a fag until a rumor went around that William was trying out for the basketball team. Amy heard that William was sitting at the jocks' table during second lunch period though his social niche still seemed undetermined. Near the end of class, Madame Sparks divided the students into small groups to converse exclusively in French on an assigned topic.

"*Aimée!*" Madame Sparks shouted. She pointed at William's group. "*Ici avec Guillaume, Claude et Marie.*"

The assignment was to conjugate several irregular verbs in the past, present and future.

"Okay, does anyone know what they're doing?" Butch or *Claude* asked.

The Bulgarian

For a minute no one said anything. William slouched deeper in his seat. Without a word Amy opened her notebook to a clean sheet of paper and began writing furiously. She was aware the other members of the group were staring at her but she couldn't stop herself. She quickly finished the assignment, ripping it out of her notebook with a grand flourish. Unsure why everyone was laughing, Amy laughed too. Butch and Teresa put their heads on their desks, facing each other, and started to whisper: "*Voulez-vous couchez avec moi ce soir?*" leaving Amy and William to stare at each other from across their desks. Amy waited hopefully for William to say something, but he just yawned without covering his mouth. When the bell rang Butch, Teresa and William left without even looking at her. Amy turned in the assignment, signing all four French names.

Later in the restroom, Amy stood in front of the mirror full of anxiety. She examined her crowded teeth for traces of food. She was almost fifteen. Her father had promised to pay for orthodontic work for her and her sister, Maryanne, but lately he had grown spiteful. Her mother and father had been separated for years, but only officially divorced recently when her mother started living with Zvetan Dimitrov, a Bulgarian coal truck driver. Zvetan, or "Steve" as he liked to be called, escaped from Bulgaria and fled to Greece, then to Italy. He was a refugee in Italy for over a year before joining some cousins in the U.S., who had started a coal truck business in eastern Kentucky of all places. Her mother had dated other men, but until Steve she hadn't lived with anyone except Amy's father.

Since Steve had moved in, her father often failed to send the child support checks or intentionally mailed them to the wrong address. When her mother told Amy and Maryanne that Steve was moving in, she said they were going to be married soon, but later confessed there was a problem. Steve was still married to his first wife and had two sons about the same age as Amy and Maryanne, who lived back in Bulgaria behind the Iron Curtain. Her mother, Barb, had grown up Methodist but hadn't been inside a church in years. Barb didn't believe in living in sin with men, but she had made an exception for Steve due to communism. Most of Steve's faults, which Amy had carefully catalogued—his fornicating and shameful atheism, bad taste in clothes and music, and poor personal hygiene—could be attributed to communism one way or another.

At home Amy lay on her bedroom floor obsessively replaying the scene from French class in her head. She saw herself hunched over the notebook as the other kids stared at her. She bit her knuckles forcefully to punish herself. She looked at her hand but it was not bleeding. She bit it again, but couldn't make herself bleed. When she heard Steve's sputtering, muffler-less Volkswagen coming down the street, she locked her bedroom door and blasted Billy Joel.

The next day in French class, William was wearing a shirt so nice, it would forever set him apart from the other guys at school who wore t-shirts, jeans and flannel shirts. The shirt was slate blue, with a sheen that added another dimension of color when he moved. His Calvin Klein jeans were new and he wore a brown leather belt that matched his Sperry Topsiders. Just before he sat down in front of her, he whispered, "*Bonjour, Aimée.*"

"*Bonjour, Guillaume,*" she whispered back, thrilled and breathless.

When Madame Sparks began speaking, there was an audible groan mixed with the sound of notebooks opening and students, reluctant and sleepy, settling down to work. Amy stared at the back of William's head while Madame Sparks discussed the field trip to Columbus, Ohio, where in a month, members of the class who cared to go and whose parents could pony up the money would lunch at *Ma Maison*, a fancy French restaurant in downtown Columbus, and tour historic German Village and stay overnight at a Holiday Inn. At *Ma Maison* they would view a live *croissant*, and choose between *coquille St. Jacques* or *coq au vin* for lunch. Most importantly, they would be excused from an entire day of classes.

Columbus was a long, tedious drive through southern Ohio, much of it on old two-lane highways that ran through one dinky town after another, towns like Portsmouth, Waverly and Chillicothe. Amy made the three-hour trip several times a year when they visited her aunt who lived in Akron. As Madame Sparks droned on, Amy imagined romantic scenarios in which she sat next to William on the bus and they talked intensely about their lives, oblivious to everything and everyone around them. By the time they arrived at *Ma Maison*, they would be holding hands. When the bell rang for first lunch, Amy gathered her courage and poked William lightly on the shoulder.

"*Oui, Aimée?*" William turned to face her. His coloring was different from the local fair-skinned Scotch-Irish kids. His skin had a slightly olive tone, and his hair was nearly black, almost like Steve's.

"Are you going on the field trip?" she asked. She was trying not to smile and reveal her extra teeth, her "fangs," as she referred to them.

"*Vas-tu à Columbus, Ohio, Aimée?*" he asked, using a deep voice.

"*Je ne sais pas, mais je pense que oui,*" she said. "*Peut-être*, maybe," she added feebly, trying to imagine how she might scrape together the money for the trip between her warring parents.

William looked at her like she was crazy.

"God, I'm fucking starving!" William said. "Got anything to eat in your bag? An apple or something? *Une pomme? J'ai faim.*"

"*Non*," she said. "*J'ai rien.*" She tried hard to think of something else to say in English or French. "I don't have anything to eat."

"What's your real name?"

"Amy."

The class quickly cleared out. Amy stood and gathered her books and papers. They walked out of the mobile unit together. Outside it was sprinkling, but Amy walked slowly hoping to linger next to William as long as possible.

"We don't have any other classes together, huh?" William asked. Before she could answer, he squinted upwards toward the sky and moaned, "Fucking rain. My hair is going to frizz." They shuffled along towards the main building in silence. "I'm like in the dumb-ass level of everything. You must be one of those smart kids," William said. "Are you in the AP classes?"

"Yeah," Amy said, hoping he was impressed.

"What college do you want to go to?" he asked.

She had never thought about it. "Maybe University of Louisville?" she guessed. "Maybe."

Tiny drops of water hit her cheeks when she looked up at him.

"I'm such a moron I probably won't get accepted anywhere good," he said.

"No," Amy reassured him, "you're not."

"Yeah, I really am. I was held back a year when I was in second grade."

Amy shrugged as if practically everyone was held back a year in school at some point in life. They were not moving, just sort of lingering around the door to the main building.

"The other day," William said, "when you wrote out that assignment all at once, I thought you were going to have a convulsion before you finished." William laughed as he opened the door to the building for her. The hall was empty. They were going to be late. "Well, here's my class," he said. "Seeya."

Amy spent the rest of the day in a state of blissful distraction. During class changes she looked for William and once saw the back of his head, but didn't manage to speak to him again the rest of the day. She didn't realize the bus ride home was nearly over until it stopped at the elementary school and Maryanne, who was in sixth grade, sat down beside her. When the bus approached the subdivision of small, nearly identical new ranch homes, Amy and Maryanne stood and exited. Last year, after renting in various apartments in town since Amy was a baby, her mother bought a house with the help of an FHA loan. The yard was still mostly dirt with patches of straw and fresh grass sticking out here and there. Amy's wonderful day abruptly ended when she saw Steve's old Volkswagen sitting in the carport.

"It's home early," Amy said to Maryanne.

Maryanne fumbled through the mailbox at the end of the driveway. "Still no check from Dad. Mom's going to be on the warpath," she announced. "A letter for Steve."

Steve's tools were strewn across the driveway. He was banging metal against metal, an unpleasant sound Amy was sure she would associate with him the rest of her life. He looked up.

"Hulloo!" he burst out.

When Steve smiled you could see that some of his teeth were covered in metal. He was thin and not very tall with dark skin and eyes, and black hair with flecks of gray. He cultivated a cartoonish thin mustache that turned up at the sides, and if he had just washed his hair, a rare event as far as Amy could tell, his long, dark bangs hung in his eyes. Otherwise he slicked the bangs back with water or his own head grease. Amy couldn't tell which. By her estimation, he only showered once a week though her mother insisted he showered at the truck stop every day. Steve wore his standard plaid flannel shirt, Wrangler jeans and his cherished leather loafers that he bought in Italy just before departing for the U.S. He barely spoke English, but her mother bragged he could speak other languages like Italian and Russian.

"For you, Amy, how was school? For you, Maryanne, how was school?" Steve pronounced each syllable carefully.

"Fine." Maryanne and Amy paced awkwardly, not wanting to talk to Steve, who was always eager to practice his minimal English.

"I fix car," he said, proudly, slapping the roof of the green Volkswagen Beetle for emphasis.

"Again?" Amy asked, trying to sound as unimpressed as possible.

"Yes. How you say? It is uh was uh break—" Steve pointed at the ground.

"Broken down," Amy said.

"Brroohhking down," he tried. He smiled broadly, revealing his metal teeth again. He looked at Amy hopefully.

"BRO-KEN DOWN." The girls corrected him loudly and without sympathy.

"So hard, English," he said, clearly discouraged. "I cook. Go. Eat." Steve waved them away. Maryanne gave him the letter. Steve looked at it and quickly stuffed the envelope in his back pocket as if it were a secret.

Inside Amy recognized the smell of moussaka, her mother's favorite of Steve's exotic dishes. Amy stomped through the house to her room and threw her books and bags on the floor and went back to the kitchen for a snack. As she passed her mother's bedroom she tried not to look inside. She hated the sight of Steve's ugly things sitting next to her mother's. Steve came into the kitchen from the carport. He took the moussaka out of the oven and put in another dish.

"Baklava," he said. "You like?"

"Yes!" Maryanne said enthusiastically.

Amy liked Steve's baklava too, but she wasn't about to give him the satisfaction of telling him so.

Later that evening when her mother came home from her bartending job, she was ecstatic that Steve made moussaka and baklava. She kept rubbing Steve's shoulder and repeating, "It looks delicious!" Repulsed by the PDA, Amy skipped dinner except for a piece of baklava. She sulked in her room while writing William's name over and over. In the evenings Steve like to have a shot or two of vodka and listen to his weird Gypsy music. He would dance around the living room, kicking his legs out like a Russian. Her mother and even Maryanne thought this was adorable, but it completely ruined Amy's television schedule, especially if he invited his Bulgarian cousins or friends over. The bunch of them would sit around talking in Bulgarian, laughing and listening to their horrible music all evening. Because Amy's father was an alcoholic, her mother never kept booze in the house; the sight of it was something the three of them associated with bad times. Since her mother met Steve, however, most of her rules had flown out the door.

Amy's mind alternated between thoughts of making out with William and seething about Steve when suddenly the Gypsy music stopped. There were footsteps coming quickly down the hall. Maryanne's bedroom door closed abruptly. In the living room, which was next to Amy's bedroom, she could hear Steve's voice, but it sounded funny, like he was moaning. She opened the door and listened. She spied Steve sitting on the couch with his head in his hands. His back was shaking. Her mother was sitting next to him with one arm around his shoulder.

"For why I did this?" he cried, staring sorrowfully into space. He mumbled something about "his boys" and pounded the armrest of the couch with his fist. Her mother tried in vain to soothe him. He said, "My boys! My beautiful boys!" a few more times and pounded the armrest again. Then he put his head in his hands and sobbed loudly.

Once Steve had shown Amy photographs of his sons, Nikola and Ivan. They were dark-haired boys who looked like Steve. Until now Amy hadn't thought about how Steve's wife and kids got along without him or how they felt about his departure. She wondered if Steve sent them money somehow or had just left them there in Bulgaria to fend for themselves.

Steve had been in the United States for about a year when her mother met him at a truck stop across the river in Ironton, Ohio. Steve and a half-dozen newly arrived Bulgarians worked for a man named Stefan, "the big one," they called him, who ran the coal truck company with his son, "little Stefan." Her mother's cousin Jeri, who waitressed at the truck stop, was dating "Mike," reputed to be the best Bulgarian in the bunch because of his nice clothes and good manners. At the time, Steve was living in an apartment with two roommates, Mike and another Bulgarian named "Bob." When her mother and the girls went to help him move, a process that took all of fifteen minutes, Amy and Maryanne waited on an old couch that smelled like motor oil while Steve and her mother packed his things in the bedroom. Bob and Mike sat at the kitchen table, smoking and speaking in Bulgarian. Their conversation had unusually long periods of silence yet they were staring at each other intensely. Neither man was smiling. Steve and her mother emerged with the two boxes and a duffel bag. Amy carried a box to the car. It contained an electric alarm clock with a cracked face; basic toiletries and some warped record albums including *The White Album* by The Beatles and several albums of Gypsy music. From the kitchen table, Bob and Mike waved and said, "Goodbye," in careful English.

The next morning in French class, William was wearing a Stanford University sweatshirt with jeans and a new pair of Nike tennis shoes. Amy waited for him to say hello before he sat down, but he didn't.

"*Bonjour, classe!*" Madame Sparks began.

When the class ended, Amy stayed seated. William stood and stretched from side to side so that his sweatshirt lifted up and Amy could see the line of dark hairs that trickled down from his navel into his jeans. When he finished stretching, he picked up his book and a dozen or so blue envelopes fell on the floor. He handed one to Amy.

"What's this?" Amy looked at the envelope. Her name was written on the front in large, beautiful handwriting.

"An invitation. My mom is forcing me to have a party so I can get to know people. She keeps saying—it's a mixer! Like I have any friends here." Amy started to open the envelope but William stopped her. He pushed her arm down and hung on to it. "Don't open it now. I feel like an asshole handing out these stupid blue envelopes. Of course, she had to pick the light blue invitations. Everyone is going to think I'm gay now."

"When is it?"

William was still holding her arm, sending electrical currents through her body.

"Two Saturdays from this one at seven. Can you come?"

"I think so," Amy said, already worrying about what she would wear.

"You'll be the only one probably," William said. He seemed relieved that she was coming but not that excited. He let go of her arm. "Make sure you call my mom and tell her you're coming because she's afraid no one from Big Sandy, Kentucky, knows what R.S.V.P. means."

At lunch Amy sat with a table full of smart kids. They were an average bunch, respected for their brains, but otherwise, invisible.

Since Amy changed schools last year, Cindy Tolliver had become her best friend thanks to shared AP classes and an interest in preppy fashion. Not long ago, after swearing Cindy to multiple layers of secrecy, Amy told Cindy about Steve. She was the only person Amy had confided in. After they ate lunch, Cindy and Amy sat in the gymnasium analyzing the subtext of her brief conversations with William. Amy showed Cindy the invitation.

"You should R.S.V.P. not less than forty-eight hours prior to the party, I think, but I'll ask my mom to be sure," Cindy said. "I think you should wear something formal like a dress or a skirt."

Later that evening she phoned her father to ask him to take her shopping the following weekend. To reach him, you had to call the V.F.W., "his office," her mother called it. He called it "the club."

The man who answered dropped the phone and it banged against something hard several times before her father picked up. In the background, men were yelling over loud country music. First, she asked how he was doing, what he had been up to lately, and how his mother, who lived in the old folks home, was doing. Her father answered in short sentences. After determining that he was sober enough to remember the conversation, Amy strategically eased into the discussion of money and clothes. He was immediately irritated.

"Why don't you have Comrade Steve buy your clothes?"

Amy waited for the usual Steve tirade to pass. Finally, Amy heard her father take a long drag off his cigarette and exhale.

"What's it for again?"

"A school function."

"What kind?"

"A school party."

"Hmm. What's your mother doing? She out with the Comrade?"

"She's at work," Amy said, frustrated, but careful not to piss him off. While they spoke she visualized her father slumped at the bar with his cigarette and shot of bourbon, the phone pressed to his ear.

"Tell your mother to drop you at the club Saturday morning."

Several days passed at school uneventfully. Amy monitored William's interactions with Madame Sparks to see if he turned in his fee and permission slip for the field trip. At the end of each class, William dutifully returned the pencil she loaned him, one of a half dozen Amy carried especially for him. Today William had fallen asleep in class. His head bobbed up and down. He had nearly fallen out of his chair.

"Well," she ventured.

"Well, what?" William asked.

"Are you going on the field trip to Columbus, Ohio?" she asked, trying to sound like she didn't care one way or the other.

"What the hell's in Columbus, Ohio, besides the stupid *Ma Maison* place?"

"It's sort of a big city around here, I guess," she said, regretting she had asked.

William shook his head. They went outside. "L.A. is a big city. God, I hate this fucking place!" William said bitterly. "I feel like I'm living in a *Beverly Hillbillies* episode."

Me too! Amy thought. In her *Beverly Hillbillies* scenario, she immediately pictured Steve as Jethro, wearing a gingham shirt and blue jeans tied at the waste with a rope.

"I'm taking first lunch today because I have an orthodontist appointment and I have to leave early," William explained.

"Really?" Amy said. "I'm in first lunch."

"Can I sit with you? I feel so pathetic being the new guy all the time," William said.

"Yes!" Amy said, forgetting to sound nonchalant. "Do you want to sit alone or with my friends?"

"You have friends?"

"Yes," Amy said, failing to pick up on the joke right away.

"Kidding!" William laughed. He punched her arm playfully.

At lunch Amy waited by the cafeteria doors. She stood at both entrances for ten minutes each, but William didn't show up. Cindy and the gang kept motioning for her to sit down. Finally, Amy conceded and joined her group. She was opening her lunch bag when Cindy yelled, "There he is!"

William stood at the entrance of the cafeteria looking terrified. Amy waved him over. He walked across the large noisy room, crouching down as if he were dodging gunfire or trying to make himself smaller. He grabbed a chair and quickly sat down beside Amy.

"This is William," she said proudly.

Everyone started talking to him at once, asking questions Amy had longed to ask for weeks. Only fifteen minutes of lunch period were left, and Cindy was dominating the conversation with William. They were talking about shopping and clothes, one of Cindy's favorite topics.

"Yeah, my mom got this sweater at," he said, touching the blue wool sweater he was wearing. He stopped suddenly mid-sentence and stared at Amy's lunch. "Gross! What are you eating?"

"Vienna sausages," Amy said, embarrassed. She held the dripping mini-sausage and saltine sandwich between her fingers mid-bite.

"Vyy-eenneee sausages!" Everyone corrected her proper pronunciation.

"I've never even seen those before!"

"Vyy-eennee sausages with crackers are good!" Dreama said. "You should try one!" She held up a tiny can of her own. "Want one?"

"Mm-mm," Todd said. "Guess they don't serve those in California!"

When William resumed his conversation with Cindy about his sweater, Amy shoved the rest of her lunch back in the brown paper sack. The other kids were cowed a little by William's cussing, especially Todd and Brad, who were staunch Southern Baptists and leaders of a Christian prayer group that met every morning before school started. Todd and Brad took turns reading The Daily Devotion, a passage from the Bible, over the school intercom every day. Cindy and Dreama were moderately religious, never cussed and often participated in the morning Bible study. William confessed that he had not made the school basketball team.

"They told me I could be a substitute," he said, "but I'm not running my ass off at practice every day just to sit on the bench every weekend. They even wanted me to share a uniform with some other loser who didn't make the team. I'm not that desperate! Fuck!" Everyone laughed but Todd and Brad. "But I'm playing basketball with a bunch of nerds at my church," he added.

Todd asked, "Which church?"

From the look on Todd's face when William said, "Presbyterian," he might as well have said he didn't go to church at all.

"We play other church teams," William continued. "I take tennis lessons, but that's about it for extracurricular activities unless you count watching TV and jerking off."

The entire table went silent. Todd cleared his throat loudly and raised an eyebrow in Brad's direction. Brad's eyes nearly popped out of his head. Then, much to Amy's surprise, Cindy and Dreama cracked up.

"What? Like I can't say jerk off?" William asked.

Todd said, "William, there are ladies present and some of us are Christians."

William elbowed Amy. Amy knew Cindy's radar for all things preppy would pick up on "tennis lessons." Sure enough, her next words were. "I love tennis. Where do you play?" Cindy was blushing, trying hard to keep a straight face. Dreama put her head down on the table and shook with laughter. Todd and Brad, in protest, began to gather their things. Amy had not managed to say anything since "Vienna sausages."

"I'm having a party in a couple weeks," William said. "I'll give Amy the invitations." The bell ending first lunch rang. "Amy's coming to the party, aren't you?"

"Yes," she said. She was sure there was something else to say, but she couldn't think of anything.

"Maybe we can all ride together," Cindy suggested.

Amy thought William might walk out of the cafeteria with her, but he picked up his books and said, "Gotta run to my orthodontist appointment. I lost my fu-" he stopped himself. "My retainer." The social interaction with her friends seemed to energize him. He turned and waved as he left the cafeteria. Cindy, Dreama and Amy waved back.

On Saturday Steve woke early and started dragging things around in the kitchen, waking everyone. He was setting up shop on the carport again. He carried a space heater outside and moved his various tools, extension cords, flashlights and pieces of his car's engine around on the driveway. Her mother went outside with her coffee. Something weird was going on between them. Although there was frost on the ground, her mother was only wearing her pink bathrobe and matching slippers. She looked tired and sad. Her long salt-and-pepper hair flopped messily to one side of her head. Steve seemed to be ignoring her as she followed him around the carport, trying to talk to him.

Big Sandy

At eleven Amy called her father at the motel where he lived but there was no answer. She called every fifteen minutes but he didn't answer until one. Amy could tell he had a bad hangover.

"We have to do this today?" he asked.

"Yes, you promised."

"I don't recall promising anything. I agreed to do something under duress one might say."

"Are you coming or not?" Amy asked.

He was silent for an excruciating minute.

"Have your mom drop you at the club at two-thirty." Her father hung up.

Her mother cried the whole way to the V.F.W. While they were waiting for Billy to arrive, her mother dropped a bombshell. Steve was moving to Queens in New York.

"When?" Amy asked, trying not to sound thrilled.

"As soon as he gets that old car fixed."

As far as Amy could tell this might be never, but there was hope. Amy tried to postpone her joy until her mother was out of sight. She maintained the same tight-lipped anxious expression she always wore. Her mother continued to cry.

"I don't understand," Amy said. "He has a job and cousins here. Why is he moving?"

"He misses his kids," her mother choked out. "He doesn't want to get married."

"What's in New York then?"

"His sister and her husband. She's a parking lot attendant in

Manhattan. She thinks she can get him a job." Her mother blew her nose several times. "Driving coal trucks makes him nervous and Big Stefan is cheating him out of his pay."

Steve had a sister who lived in the U.S.? None of it made sense, but Amy was so worried her father was standing her up, she couldn't concentrate on the Steve problem right now. Just then, her father's LTD pulled up beside her mother's Corolla. Billy got out and shuffled over. He stood beside her mother's window. He looked awful. His hair was wet. He had tiny pieces of bloodstained toilet paper stuck to his chin where he had cut himself shaving.

Her mother rolled her window down. "Stop mailing the checks to the neighbors," she ordered.

"What's the matter with you?" he asked. "You been crying?"

Her mother started the car. Her father leaned in close to her mother's face. "Wait a minute, Barb. What's wrong?"

Her mother stared straight ahead. "Nothing." No one said anything.

"The Comrade not treating you right? Want me to kick his commie ass for you?"

Her mother put the gear in reverse. "Go on, girls." They climbed out. "Drop them off at the house when you're done with dinner."

When her mother's car was gone, there was an empty parking space between the girls and their father. Amy yelled, "C'mon! The stores are going to close at five! Let's go!"

There was no mall in Big Sandy, just a few locally owned stores and not a lot to choose from. They had a little over an hour. As the lights of the store were going out, Amy finally decided on a tartan plaid wool kilt and a navy blue turtleneck. Her father sat in a chair in the corner, snoring. He was wearing jeans and a sloppy-looking sweater and leather loafers not unlike Steve's Italian ones. He paid for the clothes without saying anything, but once they were in the car he complained about how expensive everything was. Amy tried to explain as gently as possible how badly she needed the outfit for the school function.

"Yeah, I need clothes too," he said. "Nobody buys me clothes."

Her father continued to complain, but meeting no resistance from the girls, finally gave up and tuned the radio to a local high school basketball game. By now it was raining. They drove the rest of the way in silence. He dropped them off at the end of the driveway. The girls muttered a perfunctory "Thank you" and ran into the house. Her father skidded off angrily.

By Sunday afternoon Steve had stacked a few boxes against the wall in the kitchen. Her mother refused to get out of bed. Amy tried on her new outfit complete with tights, penny loafers and a headband. She wasn't sure the length of the kilt was right, but much to Amy's frustration, her mother couldn't be bothered for measuring or sewing right now. She was too depressed. Amy was standing before the bathroom mirror when she heard a crash and her mother wailing. She ran into the kitchen to find her mother on the linoleum floor, clinging to Steve's leg as he dragged her across the room. The contents of a box, including the same broken electric alarm clock and warped record albums Amy had carried for him the day he moved in, were scattered across the floor.

"For why you do this, Barbara?" he moaned. He tried to move his leg but her mother had a death grip on it. "For why you make me feel so bad?"

"Mom, get up," Amy said. "C'mon."

Steve began dragging his leg and her mother across the floor. Amy and Maryanne screamed at them to stop. Her mother finally relented and collapsed on the floor, face down, and started bawling. Steve made a run for the door. He tossed the empty box in the yard and jumped in the Volkswagen. Amy went outside on the carport and watched the sputtering green Beetle disappear up the street. She wasn't sure what to feel—relief because Steve was gone, regret for how badly she had treated him, or sad for her mother. The girls knelt on the cold floor beside their mother, listening to the Volkswagen backfire as it struggled up the hill, until finally they couldn't hear anything except the hum of the refrigerator.

"He's gone," her mother said.

They helped her mother to bed. Maryanne brought the "nerve pills." Her mother took two Valium and pretty soon she was out. Later that afternoon Cindy phoned to tell Amy that she was going to R.S.V.P. that very evening. Amy was still wearing her new outfit.

"I thought you said forty-eight hours before," Amy said.

"Not less than forty-eight hours before, but you can R.S.V.P. whenever you want."

Amy sulked.

"I can R.S.V.P. for you," Cindy suggested.

"No," Amy said. "I'll do it." She didn't try to hide the irritation in her voice. Amy found the blue invitation and sat by the phone in the kitchen. She took a deep breath and dialed. The phone rang four times.

"Hello?" William said.

"Hi, William. It's Amy."

"Oh, hi!" he said. He sounded happy to hear from her.

"I'm calling to R.S.V.P. to the party."

"I already told my mom you're coming."

"Oh."

"What have you been doing today?" William asked.

"Not much," Amy said, recalling the sight of her mother clinging to Steve's leg as he dragged her across the floor. His sad possessions and albums of Gypsy music were still scattered everywhere.

"I'm not going to Columbus," William said.

"Why?"

"Just seems stupid," he said. "Driving three hours on a bus just to go to lunch at some restaurant."

There was a long silence.

"Well, see you Monday," he said. "Bye."

After she hung up, Amy and Maryanne watched television for several hours. Her mother had not emerged from her room all day. They took turns checking on her to make sure she was still alive. It was close to eleven when Amy thought she heard the familiar sound of Steve's backfiring Volkswagen approaching the house. Maryanne and Amy looked at each other and listened a few seconds more to be sure. Maryanne jumped up and looked out the window. Then she ran down the hall, yelling, "Steve's back! Steve's back!" Steve unlocked the kitchen door. He nodded at Amy as he entered the living room and headed to her mother's bedroom. As soon as Steve closed the door, Amy felt a confusing combination of relief and irritation. The girls stood outside their mother's bedroom door and tried to hear what Steve and her mother were saying. They did not seem to be arguing. When Amy woke the next morning, Steve's car was still there. Her mother and Steve did not emerge from the bedroom until the afternoon. Amy, annoyed and conflicted about it all, moped in her room. At least her mother's bad mood might be over and she could hem Amy's kilt in time for William's party. It was cloudy and cold outside, but Amy and Maryanne went for a bike ride after lunch. When they returned Steve and her mother were sitting at the kitchen table drinking coffee as if nothing had happened. Amy and Maryanne didn't mention it either.

The following week seemed to pass slowly. In spite of the tense and uncertain mood at home, Amy was excited and looking forward to William's party. A week after driving off and returning later the same day, Steve was still living with them, but hadn't unpacked the boxes that were stacked against the kitchen wall. Amy was dressed in her new outfit. Her mother had styled her hair with electric rollers. When Cindy's mother's station wagon pulled into the driveway, Amy quickly ran outside in order to avoid inviting anyone in. The girls were nervous and tittering in the backseat.

William's house was a large two-story white clapboard home that sat directly across the street from the entrance of the maximum-security federal prison. Except for the parking lot and the entrance patrolled by men in unmarked white trucks, the prison was completely enclosed in metal fencing and layers of barbed wire. Amy knew some other kids whose parents worked at the prison. Their families moved around a lot and lived in prison-issued houses that looked like army barracks. Though the warden's house was a simple farmhouse-style home, it was much larger than the others. Over the hill, behind William's house and not immediately visible, was a new prison for people who committed white-collar crimes. Amy spotted William coming out of his front door. He was wearing his nice slate-blue shirt with the sheen. Even though Amy told Cindy that she planned to wear a navy blue ensemble, Cindy had chosen to wear a navy blue corduroy skirt, a pink Oxford shirt a navy blue cardigan with grosgrain trim. Cindy wore her penny loafers and an add-a-bead necklace that had more beads than Amy's.

William said, "Did you guys decide to dress alike?"

"Great minds think alike!" Cindy offered wittily, flashing a new smile.

"Hey, you got your braces off!" William said.

"Thank God!" Cindy said.

The Bulgarian

"Hi, Amy," William said.

Amy drove by the warden's house frequently, but had never been inside. The plain exterior belied its fancy modern interior. The floors were hardwood and polished to a perfect shine. The furniture was contemporary, not colonial or a matching set like Amy's furniture. The mostly working-class kids were not used to such affluence or style. They gawked at the Perrys' things and sat gingerly on the plush sectional sofas and chairs, talking uncharacteristically quietly. Large black-and-white photographs of William's family hung on the walls at the entrance. Amy studied each one carefully. She recognized William at the age of four or five running on the beach alongside two older girls, almost identical, with similar features.

"Can I take your coats and bags?" William asked politely.

Amy handed him her cloth bag with wooden handles and a navy blue cloth cover. It was the same as Cindy's, only hers had a green cover. William held the bags next to each other and shook his head. An elegant dark-haired woman appeared in a chic pencil skirt and a light blue blouse and high heels. She looked like someone from television. This was William's mother. Amy felt the gap between her and William open even further. Cindy was so thrilled to be in a fancy social setting she seemed to be vibrating. Immediately, Cindy held out her hand and introduced herself while Amy stood beside her.

"I'm Cindy Tolliver," she said, taking William's mother's hand. "This is Amy Pritchett and Dreama Fannin."

"Very nice to meet you, girls! I'm Isabella. I'm Will's mom."

Isabella had a thick foreign accent of some kind. She took Cindy's hand into her own and did the same to Amy's and Dreama's. Isabella smiled, revealing her perfect white teeth. Her eyes were dark with sexy crow's feet at the edges. Her black hair hung around her shoulders. Later it was revealed that Isabella was from Madrid.

"We are so happy to have you. Please come in." She motioned for the girls to enter the living room.

Amy found an unoccupied corner of the sofa and sat down. An oddly dressed older black man came around with a tray full of soft drinks. Later it was revealed the warden's household help were prisoners from across the street. William stood in front of the fireplace looking uncomfortable. Isabella said something to him in Spanish and he left the room and returned with a platter of cookies and brownies. William walked around the room offering the treats with a cocktail napkin, politely but hurriedly. Isabella barked something else to him in Spanish and William stood up straight. Everyone laughed. William's face turned red.

For a while they all sat around awkwardly, talking about school and local high school sports. William's father, the warden, appeared with William's gorgeous twin sisters, Carolina and Laura, who looked amused by the whole thing. The warden wore a nice dress shirt and glasses that sat at the end of his nose. His hair was perfectly gray although his face did not look old. He looked more like a college professor, not like someone in charge of a maximum-security prison.

"Hello, everyone. Good to have you here." Amy was surprised when she detected a southern accent. William's dad was from Arkansas as it turned out.

Even with several *hors d'oeuvres* and a few awkward questions about what it was like to live next door to the prison, the party did not last long. Everyone had phoned their parents to retrieve them. Aside from Amy's lunch period friends, William had invited mostly popular kids, jocks and cheerleaders, who left early to attend another party, leaving Cindy, Dreama, Amy, and Todd and Brad who had also come together, in the living room, waiting on their rides. Todd wore a horrible sweater vest over a cheap-looking tie with peach polyester pants and shiny, white dress shoes. He kept speaking in French.

"*Pardonnez-moi, Guillaume,*" Todd asked loudly, "*où est la salle de bain?*"

"The what?" William asked, clearly aggravated.

"Where is the bathroom?" Todd repeated.

"Down the hall," William said, crossly.

Headlights appeared in the window. Cindy stood and walked to the foyer to see if it was her mother. William quickly took Cindy's spot on the couch next to Amy. When William sat down he leaned his body into hers and whispered in her ear. "If that guy calls me *Guillaume* one more time, I'm gonna kick his ass."

Amy relished the feeling of William's warm breath on her neck and ear and the weight of his body leaning into hers. When Cindy returned to the living room and found William sitting next to Amy, she held Amy's eyes for a second, pissed. She sat down again near Isabella.

Isabella asked, "What do your parents do, girls?"

Amy felt her chest tighten at the mention of parents.

"My father and mother teach high school," Cindy said.

Amy didn't speak, hoping no one would notice, but Isabella turned to ask her, "And yours, Amy?"

"My mother is a manager at a restaurant."

She didn't say it was a hotel lounge across the river in Ironton, Ohio, or even mention her father who worked at the smelly coke plant in town.

"What about Steve?" Cindy asked.

Amy froze.

William said, "Who's Steve?"

Isabella looked at Amy with a pleasant, curious expression. Amy glared at Cindy. Traitor! Amy thought, wondering for a second if she had said the word out loud. Cindy was smiling so hard she looked like a demon. Mercifully, Todd came to the living room now wearing the peach polyester sports jacket that matched his pants. Everyone tried not to laugh.

"Mrs. Perry and William, thank you so much for inviting me, and for opening up your home to all of us," Todd said earnestly, already sounding like the Baptist minister he aspired to be.

William elbowed Amy. Isabella walked Todd and Brad to the front door.

"Mercy bo-coo!" he said as they walked out the door. "Thank you!"

"Of course, our pleasure!" Isabella called after him. *"Au revoir!"*

"Who's Steve?" William asked, elbowing Amy again.

"No one," Amy said, glaring at Cindy. Cindy looked away. Isabella shut the door and returned to the living room. William was just about to say something but Isabella put her finger to her lips and said something in Spanish. William sunk back into the couch and sulked, now leaning away from Amy. Another set of headlights appeared in the driveway and Amy, Dreama and Cindy rose. Cindy took the lead with the niceties.

"Mrs. Perry and William, thank you for having us. I love your house!"

"Yes," Amy said quietly, "thank you."

"You're welcome, girls! Come back soon!"

Isabella kissed everyone on the cheek. She said something to William in Spanish again.

"Thank you for coming," he said, but he didn't sound like he meant it. He shook their hands awkwardly. His hand was sweaty and limp.

Cindy and Dreama were already gossiping about the party. Amy noticed the lights inside the prison were still on. She pictured the inmates sitting around in their cells, on bunk beds, in striped pajamas. Some of her father's people had been in prison for various crimes like bootlegging and stealing cars. As they backed out of the driveway, Amy watched Isabella and William who were still standing on the porch, waving. It was dark and the car was moving away from the house, so she couldn't see their facial expressions. They could have been smiling pleasantly or laughing at them. "What a bunch of hicks!"

On the way home, Cindy described in great and specific detail the interior of the Perry house. Her mother, Beth Anne, kept saying, "Wow! Is that right?" Amy didn't say a word until the station wagon was in the driveway. "Amy," Beth Anne began tentatively, "does the Bulgarian gentleman still live with you?"

"Yes," Amy said flatly, "but he's moving soon." She hopped out of the car and shut the door. "Thanks for the ride." She walked quickly towards the house.

"You're welcome!" Beth Anne called. "See you soon!"

Inside, Steve and her mother were sitting on the couch, watching television. Her mother's head rested on Steve's shoulder. "How was the party?" she asked.

"Fine," Amy said. "You should see their house."

"Fancy, huh?"

Amy stood awkwardly in the middle of the living room. She wanted to talk to her mother but not with Steve around.

"Rich people?" Steve asked, squinting suspiciously.

"Sort of."

Her mother and Steve continued to watch television. Amy went to her room to change. She heard the phone ring and was surprised when her mother knocked on her bedroom door.

"For you. It's a boy," her mother said, eyebrows raised.

Amy went to the kitchen and put the receiver to her ear. "Hello?"

"What's the big deal about this Steve character?"

"Nothing," Amy said. She was stunned and elated to hear William's voice.

"Come on! Is he like your mom's boyfriend? Is Steve her luuuh-vuh?"

"He's her boyfriend, I guess," Amy conceded. The word lover in relation to Steve and her mother made her cringe. "He lives with us."

"Edward isn't my real father either," William said. "I mean, we call him dad, but he's my stepfather."

Amy was shocked. "Your mom is divorced?"

"I don't know all the details. I was really young." He changed the subject. "The party sucked. I bet everyone thinks I'm such a loser."

"Your house is really nice," Amy said.

"You should have seen our house in California. It was a lot nicer than this one. What's up with that Jesus freak, Todd? I really wanted to kick his ass tonight." William exhaled loudly. "Yeah, if it weren't for Edward, we would be living in some horrible apartment. My mother was Edward's secretary a long time ago. Can you believe that? What a cliché, huh? He's like her slave now. He's madly in love with her."

"She's really beautiful," Amy said. "I can see why."

"Yeah, she knows it too," William agreed. "They do it like every night."

Amy had no idea how to react to such a comment.

"Steve is Bulgarian," Amy said. She was ready to confess everything now. "He escaped from Bulgaria, from behind the Iron Curtain."

"What! How?"

Her mother came into the kitchen and looked at her. Amy covered the phone and whispered, "It's William," and waited for her mother to leave.

"What do you mean by *escape*?"

"Because it's a communist country," she whispered.

"But how?"

How had Steve escaped? She had never asked. She imagined a scene from a movie: Cruel communist soldiers patrolling a border from a tower. Steve crawling on the ground, under barbed wire, narrowly escaping machine gun fire. She doubted it was like that.

"Steve is not his real name."

"Duh," William joked.

"What does he look like?"

Amy started laughing. They talked for hours. William told her about the places he had lived—California, Oklahoma and Arkansas. He talked about the girlfriend he had left behind in Lompoc. Finally, neither had much left to say, but they were unwilling to hang up. By now all the lights in the house were off.

"Maybe I'll go on that stupid field trip to Columbus, Ohio," William said.

The Bulgarian

"Really?" Amy asked hopefully.

"You think I should?" he asked.

Amy knew this wasn't the question he was really asking, but she had no idea how to respond to the one she hoped he was asking.

"It's just about the only fun thing we will do all year."

"Wow, this place sucks," he said. "Have you ever been to a big city?"

Other than the time her aunt took them to Cleveland so Amy and Maryanne could see Lake Erie, she hadn't been anywhere worth mentioning, but she tried to change the subject. "So, are you coming to Columbus or not?"

"Yeah, I'll go on your field trip to Columbus, Ohio, girl," he said. "Relax."

She liked the way he called her "girl."

"Will you sit by me on the bus?" he asked.

Amy debated her next move and decided to play her card. "Do you want me to?"

"You know I do," he said. "You looked pretty sexy tonight in your plaid skirt. You little preppy, you. You better wear that skirt."

"Okay," she was whispering too.

"Okay, what?"

"I'll sit by you on the bus."

"Is that all?" he asked. "What about the skirt?"

Amy wanted to go on but she wasn't sure how. William yawned loudly. She imagined him stretched across his bed, his shirt lifting up to reveal that tantalizing line of hairs beneath his navel that disappeared in his jeans.

"Beautiful Columbus, Ohio," he said. "I can't wait."

Super Freak

During History Amy always wrote Kevin a long, steamy letter. Coach Smith rambled on about Hitler's rise to power in his twangy monotone, attempting to make humorous comparisons between post WWI Germany and the current state of the Big Sandy Tigers. The Big Sandy High School football team was in the midst of a five-game losing streak that had demoralized the school. A smart aleck sitting in the back of the room asked, "Does that make you like Hitler?" Coach Smith directed the class to silently read the chapter on Hitler's rise to power and invited the football players to gather around his desk and discuss Friday night strategy.

A few weeks ago Kevin's father had given him a shiny, black Trans Am for his seventeenth birthday and it was Kevin's mission to have sex with Amy in the back seat as soon as possible. Amy began the letter with why she liked last weekend's make-out session and why it was the closest she had ever come to helping him "break in" the new car. They had parked near the railroad tracks, under a viaduct off I-23, and climbed in the backseat. Amy allowed him to unzip her work smock and strip down to his underwear. Kevin went so far as to take the condom out of the pack of three he had just bought at a gas station. What held her back? The cold? The distracting and unromantic sounds of cars and coal trucks rumbling overhead? Writing about the possibility of having sex with Kevin in his Trans Am was making her excited. She put her head on her desk, crossed her legs and squeezed hard. When she looked over, Todd Blankenship was staring at her with his wild, unkempt red hair and sleepy eyes, possibly in the middle of a sexual fantasy himself. Meanwhile, the chapter on Hitler's rise to power went unread by nearly everyone. Amy concluded her letter to Kevin with an apology: P.S. I have to work this Friday. Sorry, I will miss the game. She signed the letter: I LOVE YOU SO MUCH!!!! YOURS FOREVER, AMY and folded the paper carefully into the shape of a football.

Weekdays after school Kevin drove Amy home and they sat in the car listening to music and fooling around in the driveway of the ranch-style duplex where Amy lived with her mother and younger sister, Maryanne. In a few minutes Kevin would return to school for football practice. He cradled her in his arms and they kissed passionately. When she accidentally hit the horn with her elbow, Maryanne opened the front door of their apartment, surveyed the situation, and quickly slammed it shut. Finally, reluctantly, Kevin left for practice and Amy went inside. Maryanne was watching *I Dream of Jeanie* reruns. She was fourteen. In spite of the excellent cosmetic and fashion advice Amy gave her, Maryanne paid little attention to her appearance. Today she wore a sweatshirt with denim overalls.

"God, you guys!" Maryanne gasped. She pushed her glasses up the bridge of her nose, a nervous habit she repeated when she was excited. Amy was helping her correct it by mocking her.

"What?" Amy said, pretending to push glasses up the bridge of her nose over and over. "What?"

"Jesus, you're practically doing it in the driveway."

Amy went to the kitchen and grabbed a Tab from the refrigerator. At five-thirty, her mother came home. The three of them ate dinner on the couch while watching the news. Amy was doing dishes when she overheard her sister say, "Amy and Kevin were making out in the driveway again."

Amy screamed, "We were not!"

"Keep your voice down, young lady!" her mother yelled back.

"She's lying!"

"Am not. I saw you."

"You're just jealous," Amy shouted, slamming a cabinet door for emphasis. "You both are."

Her mother had not dated anyone since her last boyfriend, Steve, a coal truck driver. Steve had moved to New York almost two years ago. Shortly after Steve left, the hotel where her mother had worked as a bartender and manager closed. The hotel had been the source of a colorful social life. Her mother took a dull and even lower-paying job at the hospital where she sat in a cubicle alone all day, processing bills. In the last year she had gained twenty pounds and let her hair turn completely gray, her flashy hotel lounge clothes replaced with stretchy polyester pants from discount stores.

Her mother stood in the kitchen doorway now, pointing a finger. "You better settle down." Her eyes were bulging. "And you know what I mean. Cool it."

Recently, Amy had taken a job at a local burger and shake joint to save for college, but she spent most of her meager paycheck on clothes or eating at other fast food restaurants with friends. Tonight Big Sandy finally won the game. High school kids jammed the downtown streets, honking and celebrating. The restaurant was slammed. "Welcome to Dairy-Quik," Amy said for the umpteenth time over the intercom. "May I take your order, please?" A voice she recognized as Kevin's ordered a large burger and fries and a chocolate shake. "Please pull around to the pick-up window, sir." She removed her blue polyester beret and quickly wiped a thin layer of grease off her face with a napkin. She leaned out the pick-up window to greet Kevin and a car full of sweaty football players. She filled paper sacks with cheeseburgers and several large orders of fries. Kevin pretended to give her money.

They called the weekend manager Mr. Mike. He was twenty-seven, divorced with one child. Weekdays he attended community college where he was pursuing an Associate Degree in Business Administration. Mr. Mike sat at the cluttered desk all the managers shared, in an office the size of a closet. He spent most of his time studying. He had been a promising football athlete at one time, playing one year for a state college before hurting his knee. In spite of his dumb jokes, brown polyester pants and cheap tie, there was something vaguely alluring about him. Maybe it was the way his muscles seem to be bursting out of the sleeves of his stained, white dress shirt or the combination of his five o'clock shadow and dark hair. He stood beside her register now, bumping into her intentionally. She could smell his cologne. "Gotta do a reading, sugar, move over." The restaurant was virtually empty now except for an old man who sat in a corner drinking unlimited coffee refills. The cash register began to beep as it made its calculations. Mr. Mike loosened his tie. He stepped behind her while he waited for the machine to print a long receipt of the evening's sales. Amy could feel him checking out her behind. "Don't tell me you're in love with that guy."

"Yes," she said, turning around. "I am."

Mr. Mike stared into space and brought a finger to his chin, mocking her. "I thought I was in love once."

From behind the grill, Joe asked, "Did he break your heart?"

"See, Amy, this kind of vulgar, sophomoric humor is exactly what you need to avoid. It's obvious what you need is an older, let us say *experienced* man to show you things," Mr. Mike said, pausing for effect, "to guide you."

"Oh, yeah," Joe mumbled from behind grill. "Guide her." Joe whistled. "Hey, Mike, do I have to break down the fryer and clean it tonight or what?"

Mr. Mike ripped the long receipt off the register with a flourish. "Break that fucker down, Joe."

"Hell yeah!" Joe yelled. He banged a metal spoon against some pans as if he were playing the drums. Joe went to high school with

Amy but he was a Vo-Tech student. Their paths rarely crossed except at the Dairy-Quik.

"Joe!"

"Sorry, boss."

Anne, a quiet girl who attended the private Catholic high school, was standing at the other register, her mouth agape, unwilling or unable to participate in their lurid, after-hours banter. Anne's father waited for her in the parking lot a full thirty minutes before all her shifts ended.

"Anne, you can clock out now!" Mr. Mike told her. "Tell your father good night." Mr. Mike grabbed some chocolate chip cookies that had been sitting under the warmer most of the day. "Take him these. On the house."

"Thank you, Mr. Mike! Good night, everyone!" she called sweetly.

"Good night, Anne, dear!" Joe called sweetly back, but as soon as she was gone he said, "Say, Mr. Mike, I wanna hear more about what you're going to show Amy here. Why don't you give us a step by step, so we can all learn from you. I could use some tips myself."

Shauna, the older black girl who worked at the restaurant full time, emerged from the prep room. Shauna looked at Amy. "Girl, don't believe their stories. Neither one of them knows what they're doing."

Joe said to Shauna, "How you know what he knows, Shauna baby, huh?"

"You know how I know," Shauna said. "Shut up."

Super Freak

"You sure know a lot, Shauna baby," Joe said.

Shauna grabbed a broom and stuck the end of it in Joe's butt. "Shut up."

They started wrestling with the broom and slipped and fell on the greasy floor, screaming and laughing. Mr. Mike charged out of his office with pretend outrage, trying hard not to laugh himself. Joe got up and dusted himself off. Shauna disappeared in the back. Rumor was Shauna and Joe had sex in the pantry one night. Someone found a used condom in the floor.

"Joe, we're closed," Mr. Mike announced. "Send that gentleman in the dining room home with a meal and some coffee and lock up, please."

"Sure thing, boss!"

Joe took the old man a sack of leftover burgers and fries and a large coffee and ushered him outside. Then he cranked up Rick James' "Super Freak" on his boom box and played it over and over. *She's a very kinky girl! The kind you don't take home to mother!* Joe sang and danced along. Shauna hung her head out of the back room door. "Hey, redneck, don't be messin' up 'Super Freak!' You ain't got no soul, Elvis." Then Shauna came out and danced and sang with Joe. *She's all right! She's all right! That girl's all right with me. Yeah!*

In the back room Amy washed and refilled the catsup bottles. She carried the heavy tray full of clean bottles to the dining room and ran around slamming a bottle on each table. Joe brought the vacuum cleaner to her. "Here you go!" Joe ran around the room putting the chairs on the tables so Amy could vacuum under them. He continued to sing, standing briefly on a table to play air guitar but quickly jumped down before Mr. Mike caught him. While Amy vacuumed, Joe and Shauna left to smoke a joint in his car. Mr. Mike came around and surveyed their work. Amy finished working behind the counter, cleaning and organizing the shelves and refilling "to go" condiments. Joe and Shauna returned from the parking lot, eyes glassy.

"We back!" Shauna yelled.

"Knuckleheads," Mike yelled back from his office. "Get to work."

"Hey, Super Freak!" Joe called to Amy. "Your boyfriend's here!"

Kevin steered with one hand and squeezed her thigh with the other. She stared out the window as they drove out of town towards the county where Kevin lived. Kevin's best friend, Otie, rode in the backseat. They sipped beer surreptitiously from cans. Kevin opened the sunroof. Otie stuck his head out the window and howled like a wolf. Kevin's driveway wound dramatically around a hill toward a mansion perched at the top. The house was all modern angles and windows. Kevin's father had taken a modest inheritance and invested in a lucrative fast food chain and now they were rich. A decorator from Lexington outfitted the interior of the house with chrome and glass and plush sectional sofas. Amy's mother and Kevin's mother Julie were classmates in high school, but Julie had gone to college in Morehead, joined a sorority and liked to put on "airs," as her mother called it. She was an attractive but unpleasant woman with frosted blonde hair cut in a Dorothy Hamill-style bob. She gave Amy the usual dirty look when they arrived. Kevin's parents were playing poker with some friends.

"Hey, kids!" Kevin's father yelled as they came in the room. His father stood to give the boys a pat on the back. "Great game!"

Julie looked up from her cards. "What's in that paper bag, Otie?"

"Cokes," Otie said.

The table exploded in laughter. "Sure kid!" a bald man yelled.

Downstairs in the family room French doors opened to a deck and an empty swimming pool. The three of them played pool, drowning out the hoots and hollers of the adults upstairs with loud music. Kevin and Otie admired Kevin's father's guns and golf trophies hanging on the wall. At twelve-thirty, Kevin drove her home. They stopped to park behind a deserted shopping center for a few minutes.

"You smell like French fries!" he said, biting her neck.

"Do not give me a hicky. My mother will freak out."

They had been dating for a year. Although Amy was still a virgin, a couple of years ago she had considered having sex with her previous boyfriend, William, who moved to Kansas. There was a lot of talk on William's part, but neither one of them ever worked up the nerve to push the relationship that far. Lately, Kevin was obsessed with having sex in his car. Amy pretended to like the idea too; but every time they attempted it, she hesitated. Kevin was popular, rich and smart. She felt lucky to be his girlfriend. She couldn't explain her ambivalence.

At home she masturbated in the bathroom before going to bed. Her sexual fantasies about Kevin resembled seduction scenes from soap operas. They always began in a romantic beach setting, with declarations of lasting love, as powerful waves crashed against rocky cliffs. There was sexy lingerie and soft music. Tonight, Kevin and Amy were on the balcony of a luxurious hotel overlooking the Pacific Ocean in Hawaii as instrumental guitar music played in the background. He was untying her silk robe when suddenly, Mr. Mike appeared on the balcony, out of nowhere, like The Incredible Hulk. He was wearing his mustard-stained shirt and brown polyester pants, grinning lasciviously as he grabbed his crotch. Mr. Mike pushed Kevin roughly aside. They fought over her, but Mr. Mike quickly overtook Kevin. Then Amy and Mr. Mike were back at the restaurant in his dirty, little office. Mr. Mike roughly unzipped her uniform and ripped off her bra. His hands moved over her as she lay down on his cluttered desk. She imagined him saying terrible things. Amy came immediately and felt guilty.

Sunday nights were always slow at the restaurant. Amy worked the drive-thru while Anne handled the front line.

"Two regular burgers with double cheese!" Amy shouted to Joe.

"Coming right up!"

On her way to pick up the burgers, she caught Mr. Mike eyeballing her from his little office.

"How about some fries to go with that shake!" Mike joked.

"How about an original pickup line?" Joe yelled.

"Wish I had one," Mike quipped. "You know one?"

The evening dragged on. Mr. Mike sent Anne home at seven and they began the closing routine early. At eight Amy clocked out and went to eat her free meal. Mike came out to examine the condition of the dining room. He tried to make light conversation.

"Where's your boyfriend?"

"In Lexington with his parents."

"We're going back to my place after the shift," Mike said. He was trying to sound nonchalant. "Why don't you join us?"

"I don't think so."

"I'll help you with your homework. We'll listen to music, have a few drinks. No big deal. I'll take you home."

Amy said no again, but at the end of the shift Shauna grabbed her arm and dragged her out to Mike's old Honda. "We gonna show you how to party!" Shauna told her. Amy sat next to Mike up front.

"Crank up the radio, Super Freak!" Joe ordered.

Once inside Mr. Mike's car with the Eagles blasting on the radio and Shauna and Joe complaining about "white people" music and smoking pot in the back seat, she felt nervous and immediately regretted getting in the car with them.

Mr. Mike's apartment smelled like cigarettes but looked surprisingly normal and adult-like. A matching living room set with tables and chairs was neatly organized around a television and a stereo. A framed professional photograph of his toddler son was displayed on an end table, and a photograph of a younger, clean-cut Mr. Mike wearing his football uniform was placed on another. Joe and Shauna were in the kitchen blending strawberry daiquiris. Amy and Mr. Mike stood around awkwardly in the living room. There was a loud crash and screams of laughter. "Shit," Mike said. "I better check on them. Have a seat."

When they returned Joe, Shauna and Mike held frozen drinks. Shauna handed Amy a daiquiri. Mike sat in the floor in front of the stereo. Shauna and Joe sat next to each other on the couch.

"So what's your favorite kind of music?" Mike asked her, straining to find common ground.

"Barry Manilow," Joe said.

Everyone burst out laughing.

"Can we turn on the boob tube, boss?" Shauna asked.

"No," Mike said.

"Some host you are," she complained.

"You like Fleetwood Mac?" Mike asked.

"No!" Shauna and Joe yelled.

They finally settled on The Rolling Stones. Mike noted Amy had not touched her drink and offered to run out to the store for some Tab. Amy was waiting for something. She didn't know what. She looked at her watch and wondered what Kevin was doing. She noticed the couch had cigarette burn holes in it and the carpet was old and stained with some brown stuff that looked like dog poop.

"I should get going," Amy said.

"We just got here," Mike said.

"My mom will have a fit if I'm late," she said.

She felt desperate to be home.

"Call her," Mike said, touching her knee.

"I need to go," Amy said firmly. She stood and headed for the door.

Mike hoisted himself off the floor and grabbed his keys. "Okay then." Before they left, Mike gave Joe and Shauna a stern warning: "Don't drink all my booze, don't steal anything, and—" He walked over and spoke in a lowered voice.

"What!" Joe and Shauna yelled back. "Like we would do that! What kind of people you think we are?"

Once they were in the car, Mike reached for her hand. She let him touch it for a few seconds and pulled away.

"I'm dating someone," she said.

"Oh, that's right." Mike started the car. "So why did you come tonight?"

"I don't know," she said. "It wasn't supposed to be a big deal. Right?" She moved her feet in the trash on the floor.

Amy didn't live far from Mike's apartment. He drove slowly. After a while he said, "I like you." He looked at her. She sat stiffly in the cold vinyl seat. When they pulled into her driveway, she quickly hopped out to avoid a long goodbye. Her mother and Maryanne were watching television. Amy called her friend Cindy immediately and told her where she had been. Cindy asked if anything "happened."

"Nothing. Once I was there, I was completely grossed out."

But she thought about Mike the whole week. Despite her best efforts, he continued to make his way into her sexual fantasies. The following Friday night Mike sat in his office and ignored her. After they closed, Amy went to get her coat from the back room and Mike stepped in behind her. Joe had just left the building to empty the trash. They were alone. Mike stood in front of the door with his muscular arms crossed.

"Hey," he said. "I just wanted to say no hard feelings about last week."

"Okay," Amy said. She tried to get by him. Mike moved away from the door but not far enough that she didn't have to brush against him to get out. She put on her coat and waited in the lobby. Kevin was late. She stood at the door under the floodlights.

"I'm outa here, Mr. Mike," Joe yelled. "Where's your boyfriend, Super Freak?"

She shrugged. Amy watched Joe get in his car and drive away. Mike came out and stood in the lobby, pretending to straighten crooked pictures.

"Still not here, huh?" he said.

She shook her head.

"Can't close up until everyone's gone."

"I can wait outside."

"It's cold," he said. "I wouldn't let a lady wait in a dark parking lot. Is that the way your boyfriend treats you?"

"He's not like that. He'll be here."

He stood next to her, staring at the side of her face while she pretended not to notice. She didn't remember agreeing to kiss him, but as Mike came closer, she didn't move away. His lips touched the side of her cheek and then she let him pull her down the dark hallway, away from the windows into a corner. His mouth and hands were on her face and neck. His whole body pressed against hers. She decided if she didn't reciprocate, then somehow it wasn't happening and she hadn't done anything wrong. Kevin's horn sounded several times before she registered it. Amy pushed Mike away, bolting down the hall and out the door into the cold night. She ran first in the wrong direction and not seeing Kevin's car, panicked. Then she heard the horn again. She turned and ran towards the Trans Am, relieved. Mr. Mike stood alone in the dark, watching her.

Sharon Smith

Something happened to her face. Amy sat in the Student Health Center waiting to see the dermatologist. It seemed to happen overnight. Like a sudden storm, a flash flood. Something got hold of her and started squeezing from the inside out. From deep inside, a poisonous vapor wafted out of her pores forming dozens of huge ugly pimples. They weren't just normal zits; they were large cysts that filled and stayed there. Walking around the university campus, Amy felt like a character from a horror movie. A few weeks ago, she had stopped attending classes and retreated to her dorm room. Though she knew she hadn't looked or felt like this all her life, she was hopeless that her face would ever return to normal. Inside the small treatment room she waited on the doctor, a tiny Asian man who didn't speak English very well. Every week, he injected her cysts with medicine that shrunk them, but by the next week she had grown others.

She rarely left her dorm room now. Her former roommate, and best friend from high school, had moved into a sorority house and now their friendship had grown strained. Last semester, they stopped communicating shortly after Cindy set her up on a double date. It was an important formal, requiring a special dress and a tuxedo rental. Amy canceled the day before. Cindy was furious and hadn't spoken to her since.

Amy shared a room in the towers with a black girl named Monica. Monica and Amy had never attempted friendship, though there was no animosity between them. From the start it was clear that Monica only hung around other black girls from her sorority. She ate with these girls in the cafeteria and walked to class with them. Amy was grateful that Monica spent weeknights with her boyfriend and went home most weekends. Amy wanted to hide. Every morning, as recommended by her dermatologist whose every instruction she followed religiously, she had to soak her face in hot towels so the pus would come to the surface. The sores opened easily with heat. She was a person who was filled with pus. Every day there was more. The nurse ushered her into a room. Amy watched her prepare a tray. Two syringes full of the miracle fluid, cotton balls and compresses and latex gloves.

"The doctor will be with you shortly."

The summer after her freshman year, Amy worked as a lifeguard at a Christian summer camp tucked away in the hills of eastern Kentucky. Except for a couple of weekends a month, she was cut off from civilization. Busloads of screaming elementary school children arrived every week from places like Paintsville, Hazard and Harlan. The seclusion had heightened her confusion and sense of loss. When the three of them had left for college in Lexington—Cindy, Kevin and Amy—she thought they would glide into their new lives in Lexington together. But while her best friend and boyfriend attended Rush Parties, Amy spent her days standing in line at the Financial Aid Office. Cindy's and Kevin's parents visited frequently; they attended football games and homecoming events and seemed comfortable in the university environment. Beyond visiting her dorm room, Amy's mother had never stepped foot on campus. Amy's classes were disappointing, a dull but more demanding extension of high school. Because Kevin and Cindy were pre-med students, Amy was taking the same hard math and science classes with them. When she imagined college life, she pictured black turtlenecks and heavy intellectual discussions about philosophy, politics and art, subjects she was eager to learn about; but so far all she had encountered were keg parties and drunk preppies vomiting in the courtyard. She was lonely and adrift. Near the end of spring semester, Kevin went on a camping trip with his fraternity brothers and when he returned he broke up with her.

All summer she sat in her lifeguard chair, obsessing and stewing over the events of the last year, her first year in college. At night she lay on her bunk bed, swatting at mosquitoes and growing bitter and listless. By fall, she barely had the energy to pack her things to come back to school. She briefly considered attending the community college instead, but pride wouldn't allow it. Soon after Amy moved back to Lexington and into the dorm without the support of her old roommate and boyfriend, her face exploded.

"Hello!" The doctor burst in cheerfully, accompanied by a trainee, a young soldier in the war against acne. Armed only with the miracle fluid that made the zits go down temporarily—a syringe and a few alcohol swabs—the young intern and his mentor were no match for Amy's powerful pores. The doctor spoke so quickly and with such a strong accent, Amy could barely understand him. "You take antibiotics, yes?"

Amy nodded. The trainee, a tall young man, stood by the door looking uncomfortable. The doctor always smiled and bobbed his head up and down as he spoke. *Hot compress, yes?* He had very white teeth. He wore a contraption on his head that had a light and special magnifying lenses he could flip up and down. He turned the contraption on and took a long, serious look at her face.

"Yes, another one here. One here. Hmm. Yes." The doctor stepped aside and let the trainee look. Amy didn't have the energy to be embarrassed anymore. The trainee leaned in and flipped on his contraption. He took a quick look, nodded and stepped back. The doctor came at her with the syringe. He was wearing latex gloves. "You feel a little pinch," he warned her. "A little pinch." She felt him exploring the rocky terrain of her face with his gloved fingers. "Hmm. Yes. Another one here, too." Amy held her face perfectly still. Three, four, five pricks. She lost count after a while. Liquid ran down her face. She didn't know if it was pus, blood, medicine or tears. When the doctor saw that she was crying, he patted her shoulder.

"It's okay," he said. "Finished." The doctor and the trainee left.

A minute later a nurse appeared. Amy lay on the table holding cotton compresses to her face She was crying so hard she was having trouble breathing. After a while, the nurse asked her if she would like to talk to someone. Amy nodded. The kind nurse led her down a hall to Student Counseling Services. She was still holding the bloody, pus-stained compresses to her face. Then, had she fainted? She woke up in some sort of holding room on a gurney.

Her mother and sister packed most of the things from her dorm room while Amy sat on the bed and watched. They left a few items, implying she might return to school at a later date. Some girls from her floor watched her leave from the safety of their doorways. The strange, pus-filled girl was leaving.

Back home in Big Sandy, Amy retreated from life. Several weeks passed and it was clear she wasn't going back to school. When her mother went to work, Amy moved from her bedroom to the living room where she lay on the couch all day under a quilt, watching television. Her younger sister approached her cautiously, as if Amy were so fragile, even noise could hurt her. She rarely left the house. The treatments for her face continued. Her mother drove her to Lexington to see a dermatologist every two weeks. Her face was such a mess that it now required experimental medication. Every week she had to take a blood test to monitor her reaction to a new treatment for acne called Accutane. She saw a psychiatrist once a week and took medicine for her depression. At night she listened to her mother's tearful telephone conversations with various friends and relatives.

"She lost everything. Kevin. School. She had so much potential. I just don't understand what happened."

~

By the end of summer the volcanoes began to shrink, leaving holes in their wake. The dermatologist said that with years the scars would heal—to a certain extent. There were new treatments for acne scars, but she couldn't afford them so it didn't matter.

Her mother threw a fit, but Amy insisted on returning to Lexington in the fall. Amy rented an apartment with a girl whose name she took from a flier taped to a window of a convenience store near the campus. Her name was Sharon Smith. It turned out Amy knew her from her freshman writing class. On a Southern campus of some 25,000, Sharon was among a small cadre of punk rockers sporting Mohawks, piercings, black leather jackets and combat boots. Like most of the apartments in the student ghetto, theirs was run down and roach infested, but it was cheap and Amy was thrilled to be out of the dorms.

Amy stood in the bathroom doorway, watching Sharon form her freshly dyed pink hair into spikes with multiple cans of hairspray. Her real color was strawberry blonde. Two orange kittens played at Sharon's feet. The girls were trying to decide what they should major in.

"That English teacher loved you," Sharon said in her thick Southern drawl. In light of Sharon's strange urban appearance, her accent was disorienting. Sharon described herself as being from a "stop sign" in western Kentucky near the Tennessee state line. She was the youngest daughter of five in a family of conservative farmers, but had somehow found her way to punk rock, sex and Quaaludes when she was in high school. Although Sharon had been on her own in Lexington a year longer than Amy, she had made little progress in school, only accumulating a handful of credits, even less than Amy. Sharon's attention was largely focused on her tumultuous relationship with Pete, a thirty-five-year-old musician and dishwasher. Pete was heavily tattooed, smelled, and was stoned most of the time. During Pete and Sharon's frequent breakups, Sharon picked up other musicians and strangers she met at bars. Amy woke in the middle of the night to grotesque sex sounds and never knew whom she might find emerging from Sharon's room in the morning. Amy thought the punk rock thing was pointless and vulgar, but every weekend, out of sheer boredom, she went to Pete's shows with Sharon, using fake I.D.s to get in the bar. Sharon and Amy stood around in a dark alley, smoking and drinking with the band between sets. When the music began, Amy watched as Sharon threw herself in the middle of the violent, sweaty crowd.

Although Sharon had a few issues, maybe even more than Amy, deep down she was good-hearted and appreciated Amy's company. They stood in line at the Financial Aid Office together, eagerly awaiting the grant and loan money they would quickly spend on tuition, rent, posters and textbooks they would likely never read.

"Maybe you should major in English," Sharon suggested. It was true. Amy was the darling of the teaching assistant, an earnest young woman who read sections of her essays to the class and encouraged Amy to keep writing.

When Amy returned to school in Lexington against her mother's and her psychiatrist's better judgment, she thought that she would find a renewed dedication to scholarly pursuits. School would give her a *raison d'etre*. Both Sharon and Amy began the year as full-time students. After a month, Sharon dropped to part-time, and only attended one of her two remaining classes, Nutrition, because it met at three o'clock in the afternoon. Sharon usually woke at one. Amy attended all her classes and performed her work-study job, making copies and answering phones for the Chemistry Department, but except for a writing class she liked, she wasn't interested in school. For the most part, Amy's mind was still on her "breakdown" as she called it and the turmoil and memories it had stirred up. Every time her mother called, Amy took aim at her about some old wound. Her mother inevitably hung up in tears, always claiming that she knew their childhood hadn't been great, but that it was the best she could do at the time. Since her mother returned to church and started attending a divorced women's support group there, this was her new mantra.

Still, the idea of majoring in English was an intriguing one. Amy thought about it for a couple of weeks, and once she decided she was going to do it, it still took her a few more days to work up the nerve to go through with it. She opened the heavy doors of the Office Building and lingered in the crowded lobby full of people rushing to and from class. She thought of turning back, but just as she was about to give up, she saw someone from her Introduction to Literature class and they stepped on the elevator together. The girl was headed to the English Department too. If the secretary in the office had uttered one syllable in a strange way, it would have sent Amy flying down the stairs. It would have been proof of what she already knew—she didn't belong at a university. The woman led Amy down a quiet hallway to an advisor's office and told her to wait there. The door opened and a young man left. A middle-aged man wearing a tweed jacket and old-fashioned wire-rimmed glasses greeted her. He looked at her wearily.

"Another lost soul?"

"Huh?" Amy said.

He laughed. "A bad joke." He waved her into his dimly lit office. "Come in." The walls were lined with bookshelves. Classical music played on a radio. "So you want to major in English?"

Amy shrugged. "Yep."

"Sit down," he said. "Do you have your transcripts?"

Amy pulled the paper out of her backpack and reluctantly handed it over. She watched Professor Cohen's reaction.

"A bit of a rocky start," he said. Amy waited quietly as he read it and made notes. "What happened last semester? Looks like you withdrew?"

"I was sick. I was anemic and had to go home for treatment."

"Really?" he asked, genuinely concerned. "Are you better now?"

"Yes." Out of nowhere, tears welled up in her eyes. Professor Cohen looked up from the transcript just as Amy wiped a tear away.

"Everything okay?" he asked.

And then she was crying. She didn't know why. Something about the kind way he asked, "Are you better now?" like he really cared. She wished she hadn't lied.

The room was still. Amy felt Professor Cohen staring at her. She heard him shift in the chair and click his pen a few times. He waited for a moment or two, but when her tears didn't stop, he cleared his throat, stood and closed the door. He handed her an old-fashioned cloth handkerchief and patted her on the back. This gesture made her cry more. After a couple minutes she managed to pull herself together. Professor Cohen made a rough schedule of classes she was to follow for the next two and a half years. He told her to call on him any time. This incited a new round of tears. She thanked him and fled down the stairs. She found a bathroom and stayed there for an hour. Tears and snot dripped on her new schedule as she examined it. This was a plan. She was going to shape up. She splashed some water on her face and made her way back to the apartment.

That evening Sharon and Amy walked downtown to the Kentucky Theater to watch *Nosferatu*, a foreign movie her writing teacher had recommended. Neither Amy nor Sharon had ever seen one. Amy told Sharon what happened in Professor Cohen's office, how his kindness had made her cry.

"Maybe he was hitting on you," Sharon quipped.

"No. It wasn't that." The suggestion of foul play on Professor Cohen's part irritated her.

"Hmm," Sharon said. "Maybe I should major in English."

Sharon had stolen her half of the rent from the cash register at the restaurant where she worked. Amy begged her to put it back. "You could go to jail," Amy said sternly.

"Nah."

They took their place at the end of the line. Sharon lit a cigarette. A girl near the front of the line turned and waved at Amy, and before Amy could avoid it her old friend Cindy was upon her. She wore a sweatshirt with big Greek letters.

"Oh my God! I can't believe it," she shrieked. "Where have you been?" She grabbed Amy's shoulders.

"I went home for a while," Amy mumbled.

"Yes, I heard about that," Cindy said. Her sunny facial expression struggled in vain to form something resembling sympathy. She fiddled with her add-a-bead necklace, while giving Sharon a thorough head-to-toe onceover. "My mother told me what happened. She heard it from Kevin's mom. You know he's engaged," Cindy blurted out. "She's a Chi Omega."

Before Amy could register the shock of this news, Sharon butted in. "Bitch," she growled. Cindy's eyes popped open. "Yeah, I'm talking to you. You couldn't wait to tell her the news, could you?"

"Sharon," Amy said. "Calm down."

"Let's get out of here, Amy." Sharon pulled Amy out of the line and roughly dragged her down the street as Cindy and the other people standing in line watched. Amy wrenched her arm free and turned around. Cindy was still standing with her mouth hanging open.

"What do you think you're doing?" Amy yelled.

"She couldn't wait to tell you about Kevin, could she?" Sharon kicked a garbage can. She thrust both her middle fingers in the air angrily towards the theater. Cindy stood with her friends, staring. People gasped and whispered. Although Sharon would have described her behavior as punk, Amy saw it as plain old redneck. Nevertheless, Sharon was protecting her friend the only way she knew how. It was the kind of loyalty Amy had been missing, the kind she had expected from Cindy and Kevin, but on the streets of Lexington, in front of her former best friend and sorority girl, Sharon's loyalty embarrassed her.

At home, they sat on the porch eating a frozen pizza. The news about Kevin hurt but was not unexpected. After they finished the pizza, Amy did something strange; she went inside to study. Sharon looked at her like she was crazy.

"Let's have a beer," Sharon suggested. "It's my only night off this week."

Amy agreed to one, but as soon as she finished, she went to her room and found the British novel she hadn't touched in a couple of weeks. Sharon followed her inside and put on a demo tape that Pete's band made recently. Amy asked her to turn it down.

"Now you're acting like a bitch!" Sharon said. She stormed out of the apartment and was gone the rest of the night.

As Amy's dedication to her graduation plan grew, she began to meet with some other English majors in the evening who were starting a literary magazine. Sharon was jealous and dismissed Amy's new bookish acquaintances as boring. Now that she was concentrating on school, Amy had less patience for the dramas of Sharon's tumultuous life—Pete, and the various lovers she dragged in the apartment in the middle of the night, the bladder infections and pregnancy scares, the financial woes. Just before winter break, Amy sat in the waiting room of a medical office building while Sharon had an abortion.

Amy's mother came to pick her up for the break. The girls exchanged gifts as Amy was heading out the door. "Merry Christmas," Sharon said. As hard as Sharon tried to be punk, she was too nice a person, and ultimately too much of a small-town Kentucky girl, to ignore holiday rituals entirely. Amy opened her present. It was a box of Russell Stover chocolates. Amy gave Sharon a used Talking Heads album. The music wasn't Sharon's taste, but Amy hoped it might give her something new to think about. Her mother was waiting for her out front with the car running. Amy left Sharon sitting next to a miniature Christmas tree they had bought at the drug store. It was the last time Amy saw her.

Amy asked but there was no way her mother was going to allow Sharon to come home with them. News of the ugly encounter with Cindy had made its way back to Big Sandy. The day after it happened, Cindy's mother had dutifully phoned Amy's mother to tell her about it and to suggest that perhaps drugs or alcohol were at the root of it. On their way to Akron to visit her aunt on Christmas Eve, her mother lectured her. "I should have never let you move in with that girl. I knew she was trouble the moment I saw her with her hair done up like some kind of mental patient." Her mother had already talked to Amy's landlord and arranged for her to move back into the dorms for spring semester. "It's the best thing for you. You need stability."

Amy could have resisted her mother's plan, but she didn't. She called Sharon and told her. She blamed everything on her mother. Sharon shouted obscenities at her and hung up. When Amy returned to the apartment to collect her stuff, Sharon and her possessions—her black clothes, hair products, Garfield and Sex Pistols posters, the two kittens and their litter box and toys—everything was gone. Sharon left a nasty note for Amy accusing her of stabbing her in the back. There was no forwarding address.

A few months later, in her new dorm room, Amy stood before the mirror getting ready for class. As the chaos of the last two years began to recede, she hoped, with the ignorance of youth, the worst was over. Outside it was a chilly spring morning. Someone called to her through the trees. It was Brent, a young man from her writing class. He caught up to her and together they disappeared in a crowd of sleepy young people heading to campus.

Roswell, New Mexico

After winning a small cash award for some stories she wrote, Amy left Kentucky for New Mexico with the goal of writing a novel. For a year she had been living in Santa Fe with a kind lesbian couple who rented her a room in their modest adobe. Jan and Marie had all but taken her in like the twenty-four-year-old orphan she felt like. They were regulars at the restaurant where she waitressed. Jan, a former heroin addict from New Jersey, counseled other drug addicts and painted. She had a direct, tough edge to her personality that Amy admired, while Marie, a Reiki therapist from Colorado, was more diplomatic and reserved. Jan and Marie were in their fifties and had been together over twenty years. Amy couldn't help but think of them as surrogate parents. As roommates the three of them had established comforting routines like *huevos rancheros* and *The New York Times* every Sunday morning while listening to bluegrass music on the local public radio station. After breakfast they would take long hikes in the mountains. They had come to know each other quite well and were familiar with one another's struggles with work, self-destruction and dysfunctional families. Jan and Marie showed her around northern New Mexico and introduced her to other kind people as "a writer from Kentucky."

Amy met Lance at the restaurant too. The first time she saw him up close she remembered thinking that he might be on medication to control a psychological disorder. His eyes darted around wildly when he talked to you, making earnest eye contact impossible. Too bad, she thought, because he was really good looking. A copy of *America* by Jean Baudrillard was on his table. When she served him lunch he looked up and said, "Hi!" unnecessarily loudly. She laughed and he mocked her. She felt confused. With his black leather jacket, motorcycle and pretentious books, he looked like the worst parody of art stud she had ever seen, which was saying a lot in Santa Fe.

Lance started camping out at the restaurant after the lunch crowd cleared, drinking coffee and talking about the artistic projects he had on the back burner. She bumped into him at trendy cafes and bookstores, where he seemed to be flirting with her. Some days he wore coveralls as if he had just come from doing manual labor. In fact, Lance was in Santa Fe to apprentice with a well-known sculptor, but he seemed to enjoy being mistaken for the common man. When he invited her to ride up to Taos to take in some galleries with him, she revised her initial impression of him as weird and a possible womanizer to merely "questionable." Amy had never been on a motorcycle before and couldn't resist the image of herself riding in the mountains along the Rio Grande River, hair flying in the wind, with her arms around this leather-clad hunk. It had been over a year since she had been romantic with anyone. She was ready for a break in the monotonous cycle of work, tourists, folk music and homey Sunday brunches with Jan and Marie.

Up in Taos, at Caffé Tazza, they attempted a conversation about origins over cappuccinos. Lance was from Los Angeles. His father was a television producer of game shows. When she told him she was from Big Sandy, Kentucky, he choked on his coffee and spat, "Where the fuck is that!" He asked why she didn't have a Southern accent. She said she had never had one. "Well, why not? You're from there, aren't you?" he asked, irritated, as if an accent might have made her more interesting.

Lance talked about attending art school at The Rhode Island School of Design, "Rizdee" as he called it, and how he was still processing everything he had learned about craft, history and theory. He said he was trying to understand American culture and his place in it. Coming from a couple generations of Hollywood producers, he felt he had something unique and important to say about it. Amy didn't know much about art history or theory so it was hard to participate in the conversation, but Lance didn't seem to mind he was the only one talking. As he rambled on, Amy concluded his incessant talk, nervous gestures and occasional reckless insensitivity to be a cover for hideous emotional scars like her own that she hid through silence. When he finished talking about himself, his plan to travel the world in the next two years before attending graduate school and what he hoped to achieve through art in his lifetime, which he didn't think would be long enough to accomplish everything he wanted to, he stared into her eyes. "You're kind of strange, aren't you?" he asked, as if there could be an answer to that kind of question. She opened her mouth to say something important about herself and he interrupted with, "Hey! Look at the cool photograph right over your head!"

He asked what her novel was about. She rambled on about how it was a coming-of-age story about a working-class girl from eastern Kentucky.

"You?"

"A version of me, maybe."

"When do you expect to be finished?"

The idea of actually finishing the novel seemed incomprehensible, but she was flattered that Lance took her claim of being a writer seriously. "Soon," she said, "I hope."

They rode out to the Rio Grande Gorge and stared down at the river as it wound through the dramatic gash in the earth almost a thousand feet below. In the distance they could see Taos Mountain. The sky was turning a beautiful pinkish blue as the sun set across the mesa. It could have been romantic. She wondered if Lance thought it was. To her surprise he put his arm around her shoulders as they walked back to the motorcycle. He zipped the leather jacket he had loaned her and they bowed their heads together. His hands shook nervously. Then he kissed her as if he couldn't think of anything else to do. The kiss was not sweet or sexy; it was hesitant and dry. Nevertheless, this perplexing but sweet gesture endeared him to her and she decided to like him regardless of his obvious, exterior problems.

Lance had no particular schedule but he felt his time in Santa Fe was coming to an end. He wanted to move to Roswell, New Mexico, a small city in the middle of the desert, not far from the Texas state line, where he planned to live in a friend's ex-stepfather's trailer and work on his films and poetry. "Let's blow this quaint granola scene, baby," he joked, shaking a ragged copy of *The Sound and The Fury* in her face. "Look, I'm reading about the South just for you, baby." After the trip to Taos, they had seen each other every day for the last few weeks. Yet when Lance called her "baby" she still couldn't tell if he meant it romantically or if he was just joking around. His voice seemed to crack ambiguously just before the second syllable. Lance promised if she came with him to Roswell, they could live practically for free and work on their art indefinitely. Jan and Marie became uncharacteristically angry with her when she told them she was considering going to Roswell with Lance. They seemed certain nothing good would come of it.

"He's a pretentious flirt like the dozens I've seen come and go from this town for years," Jan griped. "Their main concerns are stroking their egos and getting laid."

The first time Amy invited Lance over, Jan stomped around the house, inexplicably slamming doors and cursing. Like most of the young, good-looking artists in Santa Fe, Lance reminded her of the charismatic painter who had introduced her to heroin and wrecked her life decades ago in New York.

"I admit he's young," Amy argued, "but he's basically harmless." Lance was two years younger than Amy.

"For God's sake, Amy, just be careful," Marie urged. "You really don't know what kind of person he is. He seems aggressive."

"I think his mother was an alcoholic," Amy explained, though Lance had only hinted at his mother's alcoholism. She hoped they would take a more sympathetic view of Lance if they could picture him struggling like everyone else to make sense of an unhappy childhood. "He compensates with aggression."

"That's what we're afraid of," Jan said, taking a deep draw off a cigarette. Jan only smoked when she was very upset. "That's exactly what we mean."

Amy said with more force than she intended, "Well, it's a risk I'm willing to take."

In Albuquerque they stopped to eat at a café near the University of New Mexico. After a couple of beers Lance confessed that Jan, "the butcher one," as he put it, had taken him aside and threatened to hunt him down and cut his balls off if he hurt Amy or if anything bad happened to her. He laughed but seemed subtly shaken. Though there was never any need for them, Jan also put condoms in Amy's toiletries bag. Amy forgot about them until they fell into the sink while Lance and she stood side by side in a motel room, brushing their teeth. They looked at the shiny orange squares and eyed each other nervously.

When they reached the low desert south of Albuquerque, Amy

felt she had made the right decision. The desert was vast, empty and mysteriously beautiful. She was sure she had arrived at some important moment in her artistic life. They had been heading east on Route 380 for over an hour with nothing but desert as far as she could see. She began to wonder about the trailer. Back in Santa Fe it hadn't occurred to her to ask Lance about it. When they stopped for gas in Hondo she discovered Lance had never seen the place, and had only sketchy directions. A man named Joseph supposedly had a key, but so far had not answered his phone. She worried Jan and Marie had been right. Maybe Lance really was some sort of bohemian serial killer. A few hours later they found the dilapidated trailer just outside of Roswell.

"This is it," Lance pointed. He climbed off the bike and ran around. He took a camera out of his pack and started taking photographs. "It's fucking great!"

Amy stood near the bike and stared at the trailer that looked as if it had been abandoned years ago. About a half a mile down the dirt road several other trailers sat in a clump with old cars parked around them. There was nothing around for miles except parched, brown rolling desert.

"What do you think?" Lance asked.

"Cool," Amy said, "but I don't want to stay here."

"What! Why not?"

With nothing better to do they made a movie. She walked around the trailer awkwardly. The pink strap of her bra kept slipping down her tan arm. Lance yelled, "Push it up slowly!" She did as Lance instructed, posing and smiling, she felt at the time, kind of stupidly. Months later Lance sent her the edited versions of the movies—or experimental films—they made on the trip. She watched them over and over. Much to her surprise, Lance had managed to capture something about her that had always disappointingly evaded other photographs in which she looked weighted down and literal instead of photogenic and ethereal.

They hung out at the trailer until the sun started to go down. Lance lifted her up so she could peek inside a window and a wasp flew out and nearly stung her face. They both fell on the ground and laughed. Finally, they headed back to Roswell. They ate dinner at a Mexican restaurant and checked into a Motel 6. Lance paced around the room in his underwear or sat on the edge of the bed flipping through TV channels and eating chips. Both avoided the obvious question before them until finally Lance proposed they take a shower together. She accepted. They undressed shyly and stepped into the steamy shower. They had been kissing for several weeks now, in the strange, hesitant way that Lance kissed—as if he wasn't quite sure of himself—but nothing else had transpired. They soaped each other up. She touched his nipples and he flinched. He massaged the small of her back. They stood under the hot water, holding each other for a long time. When they stepped out of the shower Amy tried to keep the mood going, but Lance seemed more interested in watching television. An hour later they fell asleep, their backs turned away from each other.

The next morning Lance called his father and asked him to wire him some money. During the night Lance had decided to ride his motorcycle to Mexico City. He had some friends from art school who were living there. He wanted Amy to come along. While they waited for the money to arrive via Western Union, they rode out to the trailer and made another movie. This time Amy held the camera while Lance writhed around on the ground naked, yelling orders at her like, "Don't point the lens at the sun!" and "Hurry, get my dick in it!" Then he put the video camera on a tripod and they both ran around naked, whooping and hollering, the broken-down wasp-filled trailer in the background and the endless desert surrounding them.

Later that evening Lance asked, "Well, are you coming or not?"

He had offered to pay her way to Mexico City and back, but even Amy knew it wasn't a good idea. Lance was weird and self-centered, and extremely immature, but basically not that bad of a guy, she reasoned. Jan's suspicion that he was just after sex hadn't turned out to be true at all. Lance seemed uninterested in sex to the point of it being insulting. Amy wanted to ask him why, but was afraid of the answer. She thought of calling Jan and Marie and asking their advice but she knew what they would say. The decision was made for her. Instead of heading to Mexico City immediately, Lance wanted to get some footage of a decadent border city like Juárez.

"And you're coming with me, baby!" Lance lifted her in the air. "Okay?" he seemed to be pleading with her. "I might need you there."

Amy melted. Of course, she would go to Juárez with him. Besides, she liked the idea of hanging out with him a while longer and riding around in the desert wearing his leather jacket, looking tough and footloose. "God, I hope I don't fall in love with you," she blurted out. She didn't know why she said this. Lance gave her a dirty look, as if she had ruined everything by bringing up the subject of their relationship.

They rode through another long stretch of desert. They left the motorcycle in El Paso and walked across to Juárez. Amy had never been to a foreign country and was immediately disoriented. Men in cowboy hats leaned against buildings, snickering and whistling at the American tourists strolling by. They found a market and Lance filmed the vegetable and fruit vendors, Mexican children and old people selling snacks and souvenirs on the sidewalk. Amy was scared to venture too far away from Lance. Neither spoke Spanish. Lance bartered with vendors in English with an accent that sounded French. "I like theees one!" He sounded ridiculous but he didn't seem to care.

Despite her protests, that night they checked into a questionable-looking hotel near the market where a prostitute and her date were checking in ahead of them. Lance wanted Amy to take a shower in the disgusting bathroom while he filmed her, but she refused. She sat on the bed, pissed. She wanted to go back to El Paso but Lance insisted on staying the night in Juárez "to get the full effect." Lance filmed her as she walked around the room, sat on the bed pouting, and stared out the window. She yelled at him to shut the camera off, but he continued to film her. Later, they walked around the seedy neighborhood looking for a place to eat dinner. Back at the hotel, sex was out of the question. After Lance went to sleep she lay on the bed, wanting to call someone, Jan and Marie maybe, or her mother whom she hadn't seen in over a year. The flimsy room was little protection from what lurked outside. All night she heard people coming and going, water running, toilets flushing, people speaking in a language she didn't understand. When it was nearly daylight Lance sat straight up in bed.

"Oh God," he said.

Then he puked all over himself. The rest of the morning Lance sat on the toilet or stood over it, puking and shitting. Amy was forced to venture out into the city alone to buy diarrhea medicine. Juárez was only slightly less frightening in the morning, but she was proud of herself for managing to find a store and for negotiating the transaction in total silence by miming. When she returned to the room, Lance lay on the bed on a bare mattress, his hair matted to his head. The room smelled like vomit and body odor. Amy stared at him, enjoying his helplessness. By late afternoon, Lance had recovered enough to walk back to El Paso. She felt relieved to be back in Texas and silently declared her adventure with Lance finished. When she asked him to take her to the bus station so she could go back to Santa Fe, Lance seemed disappointed.

"Just when I thought I was falling in love with you," he said sarcastically.

At the bus station in El Paso, he paced around in the dirty clothes he had been wearing for several days. When the intercom called her bus, Lance took her shoulder roughly and said, "Okay, last chance. Come with me to Mexico City, damn it." He was smiling. Was he laughing at her or did he really mean it? For a minute she thought she might give in, if he had kissed her or said something corny like, "We're good together," she might have. "Really, you're not coming?" he asked again. When she didn't respond, he let go of her shoulders and took a deep breath. "I'll miss you, cowboy," he said. He mussed up her hair like she was little kid.

Jan picked her up at the bus station in Albuquerque. When they were on I-25 headed to Santa Fe, she asked, "Well, how was it?" She looked over at Amy, smug. "Was it worth it?"

Amy shrugged. It would have been difficult to describe what had happened and assess its value, if any. Besides, she didn't want Jan to say, "I told you so." Amy was happy to be back in her little room, on her futon on the cold Saltillo tile floor. To her surprise Lance called her several times. He had changed his mind about riding his motorcycle to Mexico City. He was on his way to New Orleans now. The last time they spoke he was in Austin, Texas, visiting friends.

"How are the dykes?" Lance asked.

"Don't call them that."

"I managed to get away from you with both my balls intact." As he spoke, Amy pictured Lance pacing around in his dirty clothes. "Hey, I kind of miss you!" He said this as if he were astonished to discover he had feelings for her.

Amy picked up some shifts at the restaurant and effortlessly slipped back into her old routine with Jan and Marie. When Amy left with Lance, Jan and Marie promised the room to another woman but offered to cancel the deal if Amy wanted to stay on. Amy was unsure what to do next. Jan knew of a house-sitting gig near Taos. In exchange for watering plants and taking care of several cats, Amy could live in a guest house that belonged to a wealthy retired couple who divided their time between Vermont and New Mexico. She caught a ride up to Taos a few days later.

The Adjunct

The only man who flirted with her anymore was Carlos, the old Dominican who ran the convenience store on the corner, the one with the five-dollar mops hanging in the front window next to the piñatas. Amy noted this one morning as she stared at her thirty-eight-year-old reflection in the glass door of *La Tienda*. She was standing on a gritty street corner in West Philadelphia with her beloved mutt, Max. It was just past seven a.m. and she was out of milk, milk she badly needed for her most treasured of daily rituals, her morning cup of coffee. But *La Tienda* was closed, though the store hours were handwritten on an index card taped to the door. Amy looked up and down Baltimore Avenue hoping to spot Carlos, who walked with a slight limp, lumbering up the street. Until he inquired about her marital status recently, Amy had come to think of him as a gruff but kindly uncle. Now when Amy stopped at *La Tienda* for mice poison or milk, she didn't linger for conversation.

A trolley roared by. The streets were beginning to fill with people dressed for work or school. Amy pulled her vintage wool coat together as if this might hide the fact she was still wearing plaid flannel pajamas underneath. She spotted her neighbor, Mathew, and his wittily named Chihuahua, Foucault, walking briskly towards Clark Park. Even at seven a.m. Mathew looked freshly showered and stylish in his dark jeans, carefully knotted scarf and serious eyewear. Amy immediately spun around and walked in the other direction, dragging poor Max behind her.

"Max, come!" she snapped. "Damn it!"

She hadn't slept much and now she was running late for an early morning meeting with a young colleague of sorts, Dr. Casey Ryan, the English Department's new tenure-track hire. Amy taught Advanced Writing at Pennsylvania College, an expensive liberal arts school on the Main Line, one of her two jobs as an adjunct English professor. Her other teaching job was in North Philadelphia, socio-economically a world away. Several weeks ago, as per department protocol, Amy and Casey agreed to do an Observation and Exchange, a euphemism for "peer review," a strategy for improving the First Year Writing Program implemented by its zealous director, Dr. Anne Clarkson. Having taught at the college for five years now, Amy had participated in many peer reviews and they always made her anxious, but Casey's had been miserable. Casey sat in a corner of the classroom taking notes on a clipboard the entire fifty minutes. Amy had since observed Casey's class as well; he lectured on punctuation and revision with a Power Point presentation. Casey and Amy had not spoken since, though from a distance she had seen him coming and going from the English Department. Last week

Casey had sent her a terse email suggesting potential meeting times for the "Exchange" portion of their peer review. Amy chose the last possible date.

Now truly pressed for time, Amy purchased milk at the depressing gas station run by the Russians. She raced back to her apartment on the second floor of a six-unit Victorian double, sandwiched between Foucault's owner, Mathew, a gay, bi-racial graduate student in Sexuality Studies at Penn above her, and Odette, "the super," a genuine bearded lady and local celebrity activist, below. As she approached the house, Amy spotted Odette's large, round figure on the front porch in a faded blue chenille robe. Her long gray hair was piled on her head in a messy bun. Six or seven filthy stray cats with assorted disabilities—missing eyes, legs, tails—swarmed anxiously at Odette's thick unshaven ankles as she poured kibble into several bowls. Through the overgrown trees and ivy you could almost see that Odette was standing under a hand-carved wooden sign hanging from the front porch with the words "The Community" engraved in simple block letters. The Community was a land trust organization Odette founded that rented apartments and rooms for cheap in exchange for service and a solemn commitment to uphold peace and equality for all living things. The Community residents consisted of leftist activists of various stripes. They also ran a meeting space, a community garden and a donation-based vegetarian kitchen and bakery. Every year Amy planned to move out when her "peace lease" was up, but she hadn't found a comparable affordable apartment that allowed dogs. Her service was not demanding; a few hours a month she pulled weeds in the garden or worked in the bakery. She chose both these activities because of the minimal interaction with other residents of The Community, who, over the years, had evolved from laid-back vegetarian, artist, hippy types enjoying cheap rent, to strident political activists with an agenda.

"Hello, Amy," Odette said.

Although Amy had lived above Odette for years now, she still had to train her eyes somewhere above or to the side of Odette's head so as not to stare at the woman's beard. The beard was subtle, a light, reddish blonde color. It was a trick; it made you look to confirm that it was a beard and then you couldn't look away. To make matters worse, Odette's every social interaction was charged with such intensity and invasive eye contact that even the way she said "Good morning" could bring a lump to Amy's throat. Amy waved politely and pointed at her wrist as if she were wearing a watch. "Late," she mouthed. "Sorry."

While the coffee perked and dripped, Amy showered and dressed. Max, a funny mix of Dachshund and Terrier, was always able to sense her imminent departure. He followed her from room to room, his toenails clicking sadly on the hardwood floor. Max and Amy had been together for several years, since she found him abandoned on the street, dehydrated and flea ridden. "Don't guilt trip me, buster," Amy said, reaching down to give him a reassuring pat. "I'll be back soon." She gave him a treat and kissed his fluffy black head and headed out the door.

The Adjunct

Fortunately, the old Nissan Sentra started without incident. As she drove out of West Philly towards the suburbs, she cursed herself for agreeing to participate in a peer review with the likes of Casey Ryan. In his brief time at Pennsylvania College he had developed a reputation for being arrogant to the point of rudeness, but when Casey knocked on the edge of the cubicle she shared with two other adjuncts, she was taken off guard and even flattered. The young, hotshot scholar had chosen to observe *her* class. Casey, who had recently returned from a summer of research in Dublin, spoke with an annoying Irish brogue he turned on and off at will.

"Excuse me," Casey had said that morning. "Sorry to interrupt. Would you mind if I observed your class, Amy?"

His voice tipped up and down like a leprechaun's. With several prestigious publications under his belt and a Ph.D. from Penn, he was the darling of the English Department Chair. The college had granted Casey a coveted research grant. Next year he could dedicate the spring semester to his new book, which promised in the words of the Chair's blurb in the English Department newsletter, "to expand our knowledge of literary theory through the exquisite prism of a brilliant young mind shaped by the new millennium." As Casey spoke Amy noticed some pimples unattractively emphasized under the florescent lighting. After they settled on dates for the observations, Casey lingered around her cubicle awkwardly as if there was something more to talk about. Finally, he said, "Well, see you then," and abruptly left.

On the morning of the observation, Amy found Casey pacing in front of the locked classroom door. The class began at eight a.m. One of her students was sound asleep on a nearby couch. A few others stood around with coffees, staring into space. Casey wore a tan corduroy jacket that drooped off his skinny shoulders, a plain white shirt and an ugly tie. He held a clipboard and made a pointed effort to look at his watch before greeting her without smiling.

"Good morning," he said.

"Morning," she said. "Sorry, I'm late. Traffic."

She tried not to look at the clipboard. Her hands shook as she unlocked the door. She could literally feel him breathing down her neck as she fumbled with the keys. Casey marched into the classroom like a building inspector and took a seat in the corner. A couple of female students trickled in and pulled their desks into Amy's preferred teaching configuration, a circle, and left the room. When Amy turned her back to begin writing on the board, she became acutely aware of her ass in an old, tight denim skirt and wondered if Casey was looking at it. To hide it, she awkwardly held her folder full of notes behind her.

"So what are we doing today?" Casey asked.

When she told him they were winding up a discussion on the female action hero in the film *The Long Kiss Goodnight*, she could have sworn Casey looked down so that he could roll his eyes. Amy felt her anxiety rising. She tried to take deep breaths through her nose.

"So when do you cover the basics?" he asked. "Logic, grammar, et cetera?"

The Adjunct

Amy summoned her Professional Voice, the voice she never used outside of academia. "This is an advanced writing course based on a film series. The students in this class have tested out of the first semester of freshman writing. I generally address—" she stopped to swallow. She could feel the muscles in her jaw and throat growing tired from trying too hard not to sound defensive. "I generally address those kinds of issues in the grading process or in conference, and only cover specific issues in class if needed."

He shrugged and wrote something else. She was now acutely aware of the sound of his pen. She sat in the circle at the front of the classroom, trying to gather her thoughts and maintain her composure. She flipped through her notes. It was hard to make sense of what she had written the night before. Instead of actual sentences, there were underlined words connected by arrows pointing to other underlined words, and quotes from various theorists written in the margins apropos of nothing. As it had grown late, her handwriting became illegible. Her eyes moved down the page frantically trying to find a complete thought. When it was time to begin class, Casey remained in the corner outside the circle with an expression Amy interpreted as contempt.

After explaining Professor Ryan's visit to the class, Amy began her lecture. She tried to suppress a growing sense of doom. "So," she started, nervous and jittery, "how does this female character solve problems?" Almost in unison the class looked down to avoid eye contact with her. She didn't look at Casey, but she could hear his pen scratching against the clipboard, dotting his "I"s and crossing his "T"s forcefully. After an interminable thirty seconds, her favorite student, Alessandra, spoke.

"Well, she is a mother," Alessandra began.

"Yes," Amy said, hopeful the girl had more to say.

There was another long, anxious pause as Alessandra searched for the right words.

"The combination of mother and assassin is shocking for us," Alessandra continued. Alessandra lisped slightly because of a tongue piercing.

"Hmm," Amy added, nodding, encouraging the young woman to continue. Amy waited but Alessandra shrugged as if to say, "That's it." Amy noticed a couple of students glancing at each other sideways, smirking. She wondered if the sound of Casey's pen against the clipboard was growing more audible or if it was just her imagination. "Anyone else?" she asked. "Any comments on other aspects of the film?"

Amy scoured the classroom searching for a raised hand, a thoughtful face, a half-opened mouth, a finger to the temple. Finally a couple of students raised their hands and the discussion, though slow to start, began to heat up around the African-American sidekick, and continued without much nudging from Amy until the end of class. The character played by Samuel L. Jackson recalled a Stepin Fetchit caricature with the usual unresolved sexual tension between the black male and the white female lead, in this case Geena Davis.

The Adjunct

Casey grudgingly looked up from his clipboard to listen. Speaking in class during an observation was forbidden, so there was some comfort that even if Casey thought the discussion of popular films was useless, he wouldn't be allowed to say so. When class was over, he dutifully thanked her and said, "We'll follow up later." Then he marched out of the room with his clipboard under his arm.

When Amy crossed City Avenue, out of Philadelphia proper and into the suburbs, the neighborhood abruptly shifted from rundown row houses, check-cashing shops, African hair-braiding salons and Halal butchers to the well-tended lawns and old money estates of the Main Line. She briefly considered calling Casey and canceling, feigning sickness or car trouble; but she continued down Lancaster Avenue towards the college, passing expensive boutiques and investment companies, heart pounding, as if she were on her way to learn the results of a biopsy.

When Amy arrived at the entrance of the college, she flashed the only item the English Department had given her that bestowed any status upon her whatsoever—her parking pass—which had the word FACULTY written in large white letters against a red background. Casey suggested meeting at the student center food court of all places, even though, being a tenure-track professor, he had an office of his own. After trekking across the campus, she arrived at the expensive new building that housed a movie theater, a conference center, and a food court complete with throbbing bass and a disco ball. Amy joined the herd of young people entering through heavy glass doors and followed the smell of popcorn, coffee and pizza.

Mercifully, the disco ball was turned off this morning. CNN played silently on several television screens. Amy stopped to order a coffee. She spotted Casey sitting at a table. While the barista made the Americano, she watched Casey from the counter. He appeared to be dressed in the same clothes he'd worn to the observation, the same ugly tie and white shirt. His tan, corduroy jacket hung on the back of his chair. He was studying something in his notebook. When she approached the table, she saw that it was a long list of bulleted items that turned out to be his "feedback." Amy had not prepared any comments on his class—just a handful of manufactured compliments focusing on the positive that she hoped would disarm him. "You appeared confident, prepared and engaging," she rehearsed silently. "I really liked the way you—" In fact, she observed several students nodding off in the dimly lit room, the hum of the projector lulling them to sleep as he droned on about the subtleties of the semicolon. She was determined not to be critical in her comments, but to kill with kindness. Amy arranged herself at the table.

Casey opened their conversation with, "So what's up with the circle?"

"Good morning to you too!"

"Oh," he said. "Sorry. Good morning."

Amy tried to sip her coffee but it was too hot. Casey checked his watch and fiddled with his pen. He looked nervous and cocky at the same time. She took several tiny sips of coffee, looking in the other direction. Unable to bear the terrible silence, she set her coffee down, put her hands in her lap, and readied herself for the blows.

"Can we start?" he asked.

Amy nodded.

"I don't know," Casey said. "I thought the circle seating arrangement went out with the sixties."

"I think a lot of teachers, especially wom—"

She stopped herself. She didn't need to justify her seating arrangement or anything else to him. So what if he had a Ph.D. from Penn? She noted that Casey was not speaking with his Irish accent this morning and he was wearing concealing medication on his pimples.

"Well, I don't find the seating arrangement prohibitive to discussion or anything else for that matter," she said, trying to sound casual. "I thought the discussion was . . . fruitful, lively." She tried to smile, astonished that she had just used the word "fruitful."

Conceding the battle of the circle, Casey moved his pen down the bulleted list. He found a spelling error in the comments she had written on the board. She nodded in agreement. She would let this one go in the spirit of getting this over with as quickly as possible. Casey pulled out a copy of her syllabus where he had made multiple comments as well. After perusing the pages for a minute, he nodded as if to confirm something.

"What?" Amy said, trying to keep her anger in check. "Is there a problem with my syllabus too?"

Casey noted her "too."

"Hey, I'm not trying to be critical here. You can take my comments with a grain of salt." He loosened his tie nervously. "What do I know? You've been teaching longer than I have. That's why we do these things, right? To learn from each other?"

Amy waited.

"I guess," he hesitated, running his fingers through his thinning brown hair and handling her syllabus again. "I'm kind of wondering where your so-called film theory comes from. Obviously, it's steeped in feminist psychoanalytic theory. This section is called—pithily, I might add—*Mothers and Killers*."

So-called film theory? She inhaled deeply. She was weighing her response options, when something caught her eye. The couple sitting behind Casey on a raised platform in a secluded booth was French kissing. When they stopped for air their tongues retracted into their respective mouths like weird mating insects. They went at each other's mouths again and again, tongue first. The young man was stroking the woman's bare inner thigh under the table, high under her mini-skirt, shockingly close to her crotch. The woman's legs were spread slightly so that the insect man could get a better angle.

"I guess you could say I feel free to pick and choose," Amy started. "I don't feel bound by one theorist or any overarching theory. I use whatever might get the discussion going." She accidentally took a big gulp of the too hot coffee and burned her tongue and throat but swallowed silently. Casey looked at her suspiciously from across the table.

"So what did you think of my class?" he asked.

She wanted to say, "So where's your Irish accent today, Casey?" Instead she said, "It was fine, Casey." She felt drained, damp with sweat. Her tongue and throat were burning now. She needed to go to the bathroom.

He looked surprised. "Really?" he asked, almost incredulous.

The French-kissing couple shifted position. The girl arranged herself on the young man's lap. My God, Amy thought, are they going to start humping right here in the food court? Casey turned to see what had caught her gaze. Just as he looked, the couple went at each other's mouths again with their weird insect tongues. The young man held the girl's bare thighs. Casey turned to face her again and their eyes met for a few uncomfortable seconds. His pale, skinny fingers danced around his mouth. Amy looked into her coffee and ventured a small joke: "You have a keen appreciation of the semicolon."

"Indeed," he said, sighing as if this wasn't news to him. "Any suggestions for me?"

"No," Amy said. "Are we finished here?" She started to gather her things.

"Well, there was one more thing," Casey started, "but it's you know, just a suggestion, the kind of thing you can take with a grain of salt."

"You said that before."

"On the one hand your appearance is youthful and attractive, you know, with the denim skirt, boots and tight turtleneck and all."

Attractive? Tight?

"You're like the cool mom type, you know." He smiled thinking about this.

Mom?

His eyes darted from her breasts to her face.

"You have two kids, right?" he asked. "Oh, wait," he said disingenuously. "I'm confused." He brought his finger to his temple as if trying to remember something. "You're married, right?"

Surely this was not his way of coming on to her!

"Anyway," he backed up, "dressing like one of these guys—" he waved his hand across the food court dismissively, "it could work against you in terms of authority, not that you can't carry it off." After this comment he seemed to know he had overstepped his bounds. "But you've been doing this a while, so I should really shut up."

"Well, thanks for all the useful *feedback*, Casey." Amy said snarkily. She pushed her chair away from the table and stood.

"You going back to the English Department?" he asked. "I'll walk with you."

She held her hand in front of her as if to physically stop him. "No. Library."

Casey ripped some pages from his notebook. "You want to look these comments over?"

Amy reluctantly took the papers and crammed them inside a side pouch of her briefcase.

Your so-called film theory?

The Adjunct

One more time, his eyes darted down to her breasts and up again. He seemed to want to say something else, but he turned towards the table. The horny insect couple was gone.

Furious, Amy marched to the library to return some books. Then she dashed back to the gulag, the affectionate term the adjuncts used to describe the basement where the Pennsylvania College English Department housed its part-time teaching staff. It was a large cold room, divided by clusters of cubicles. There were two computer stations and some old filing cabinets along a wall. She had intended to finish grading a few papers before her next class, but she was so angry she couldn't concentrate. Instead she listened to Melinda, a young adjunct who sat in the cubicle on the other side of her, cheerfully coaching an Asian male ESL student.

Ten years ago Amy had dropped out of a Ph.D. program in English, but she was unable to tolerate or fit into any of the dull corporate jobs she had attempted after leaving the program. Additionally, she found office work and the inflexible daily routines and sterile work environments physically and intellectually numbing. She rationalized that even though the pay was terrible, and the benefits non-existent, adjunct teaching was at least stimulating, the schedule flexible, and she would be free to pursue her eclectic and sometimes unjustifiable intellectual interests *vis à vis* choosing class material. At some point she figured she would get back on course; re-enter official *academentia;* take time to research and write some essays about popular culture, feminism and class; publish them and finally obtain a full-time teaching position. Yet somehow a decade had slipped by and having made no effort to complete a single essay, Amy had been teaching freshman composition ever since, for a fraction of the pay and no benefits she would have earned as a full-time professor with a Ph.D. Being an adjunct was like what her mom used to say about living together versus marriage: Why buy the cow, when you can get the milk for free?

When Amy arrived in West Philly again it was dark. She walked quickly towards her apartment, lugging a heavy briefcase full of papers with one hand and her groceries in the other. Poor Maxie had been alone all day. Across the street Mathew was getting out of a mint-green Saab with his companions, Brian, a Korean-American law student, and Sean, a snippy web designer. All three of them generally spent the night at Mathew's apartment. Amy had no idea what the sleeping arrangements were. One night she put her ear to the wall and listened for sounds of kinky sex, but only heard electronic music. Occasionally when Mathew went out of town, Amy took care of Foucault. Mathew's apartment, though old and in ill repair like her own, was always immaculate and there were no obvious signs of a *ménage a trois*.

"Hello, Amy!" Mathew said, waving. "How are you?"

She was standing on the porch by now, digging for her keys in her purse. As the three young men approached, the air filled with the smell of cologne.

"You remember Brian and Sean, right?" Mathew asked. "Guys,

you remember my neighbor, Amy. She teaches at Pennsylvania College."

"Hi, Amy!"

"My keys are in here somewhere!" Amy mumbled, still digging. "The porch light is burnt out, damn it! I can't see a thing."

"Did you read his blog today?" she heard Brian ask in a hushed voice.

"He's so mired in a sort of old-fashioned leftist ideology which he's brilliant at in his way," Mathew responded. "I mean, it's charming. Hey, Amy, use my key, sweetie!"

Amy turned to grab the key from Mathew. She took in the sight of the three young men waiting behind her. They held briefcases and groceries packed in eco-friendly bags. Their heads glistened with hair gel. They looked and smelled as if they were at the beginning of their day, not at the end, a day Amy imagined that was full of sharp commentary and turgid discussions around heavy wooden tables. Amy unlocked the door and headed upstairs without looking back.

"Thanks, Mathew!" she called down behind her.

Max jumped up and down, excited to see her. She waited until she heard Mathew's door close upstairs. Then she grabbed the leash and headed outside again for a quick walk with Max. When she returned Brian was stepping off the porch with Foucault. The dogs greeted one another enthusiastically.

"Foo-Foo!" Brian purred. "Oh my God, they love each other, Amy! It's so cute! Let's take them to the park soon so they can have a play date!"

"Yes," she forced herself to reply, "we should do that. Goodnight."

Once upstairs she made a can of soup and sat in front of the TV. She looked at her briefcase, bulging with student papers and departmental mail she needed to read. There were phone and email messages she needed to check. Tomorrow she would deal with all of it. She changed into pajamas and tried to watch *Law and Order*. Then she ate some cereal and readied herself for bed. She tried to read.

Your so-called film theory.

She heard some rustling coming from the kitchen cabinets. Mice! She banged on the wall to scare them away. They were growing more brazen. One of them had scurried across her bedroom floor the other night as she sat on her bed grading papers. Unable to relax, she went back to her living room and collapsed on her futon couch next to her briefcase. The papers Casey Ryan had forced on her were sticking out of the side pouch. She had not bothered to look at them earlier. She grabbed them, bracing herself for another barrage of criticism, but there was no bulleted list. Two pages were blank. The third one was nearly blank except for a perfectly centered handwritten paragraph in the middle of the page, printed in tiny meticulous handwriting, a quote she recognized from *Finnegan's Wake:*

> . . . she is so pretty, truth to tell, wildwood's eyes and primarose hair, quietly, all the woods so wild, in mauves of moss and daphnedews, how all so still she lay, neath of the whitethorn, child of tree, like some losthappy leaf, like

blowing flower stilled, as fain would she anon, for soon again 'twill be, win me, woo me, wed me, ah weary me!

Amy wadded up the paper and threw it across the room. She paced from one end of the apartment to the other, not sure what to feel. Flattered? Sexually harassed? She retrieved the paper and read it several more times. Then she went to bed and fell asleep, hard, because she was deeply exhausted. The phone rang. Her mind went immediately to her mother in Kentucky. An emergency.

"Hey, uh, Amy. It's me, Casey Ryan. Hope I'm not calling too late."

She was relieved that it was not an emergency from Kentucky, but alarmed to hear Casey's tense voice. Max stirred at the foot of the bed. Amy heard rustling in the kitchen cabinets again. She sat up and turned on the light beside her bed. It was eleven-thirty.

"So what's on your mind, Casey?" Amy asked. She detected a hint of her Professional Voice in her tone. Then she realized she didn't have to sound defensive anymore. The poor guy had a crush on her.

"I hope there are no bad feelings between us," Casey said. He paused for an uncomfortable few seconds as if waiting for her response. "I may have been a bit too zealous in my attempt to observe you." He sighed. "Anyway, I'm sorry." He paused again as if he were waiting on her to say something. "I'll let you get back to whatever you were doing." He didn't mention his note.

"I read your feedback."

"God, if I offended you, I'm so, so sorry. Really."

There was not only rustling in the cabinets now, but also squeaking and what sounded like wrestling. Max jumped off the bed and went to the kitchen and barked at the cabinet.

"Did I?" Casey asked.

"What?"

"Offend you?"

He was both apologizing and assessing her reaction to the note. Was she offended? Shouldn't she be offended? She briefly debated the wisdom of entering into any sort of romantic entanglement no matter how brief or superficial at this late date, given their age difference, the fact that they worked together (like that had ever mattered), the stalled state of her life and career; she needed new underwear, a new apartment, a hair appointment, and waxing in all sorts of places. She thought back to her awkward encounter with Carlos, the old Dominican, the last time she could recall anyone exhibiting a romantic interest in her.

"*Tienes novio?*" Carlos had asked.

"*Sí,*" Amy lied.

"*Disculpa,*" Carlos said, quickly looking down.

Casey took her silence as an opening. "Maybe we should meet and talk about this," he suggested.

"Yes," Amy agreed. The word came out of her mouth almost involuntarily. "Maybe we should meet and talk about this."

Big Sandy

When Amy went home to Big Sandy, a rare event now that her mother had moved to Knoxville, she always drove by the old coke plant where her father used to work. The plant shut down in 2007 and the company was planning to demolish it. Still, Amy liked to walk along the railroad tracks and take photographs. She knew it was weird to feel nostalgic about a place soon to be labeled a "brownfield," but it had been a focal point of her childhood, like a scenic mountain range or a lovely river. The railroad tracks ran along the Ohio and Big Sandy Rivers, northwest towards Ohio and into the coalfields of West Virginia and southeast Kentucky. To her mind the rivers had been an unnatural extension of the factories that lined their banks—steel, coke, chemicals and oil. Barges loaded with coal and other goods moved up and down the Ohio River daily. When Amy was growing up, there were mounds of coal around the plant. The plant emitted a terrible smell. Fire shot out of the smokestacks and the flames from the ovens could be seen from the road as you drove by. Coal trucks ran up and down I-23, which had been christened the Country Music Highway in the 1990s. Now the plant was a ghostly, rusting, gray structure. The gates to the parking lot were locked. Weeds four feet high blocked the entrance to the Union Hall. A sign that said *Don't Be A Scab!* was still posted on the front door.

She was amazed at how her father managed to drag himself to work decade after decade, to a job he professed to hate, but clung to over forty years. It was the only consistently normal thing he ever did with his life. Other men had homes and families to tend to, and holidays, birthday celebrations and anniversaries to mark the time. Billy drifted from the motel to work, and on to the V.F.W. until he was in his late fifties, when he abruptly quit drinking. He tried to rekindle his relationships with his lost family then. One day he called Amy out of the blue and asked if she needed anything. It had been years since she had spoken to him. A week later she found a money order for two hundred dollars in the mail. She recognized the poor penmanship on the envelope immediately from so many years of retrieving and often not finding the child support checks in the Saturday mail. He had missed high school and college graduations, her sister's marriages and divorces, and funerals of close family members. Yet he began calling regularly, as if he was now entitled to all of it.

After Billy retired he confessed to being half drunk through most of the years he worked at the plant. Amy pictured him sipping from a flask he kept in his locker or tucked in a secret pocket in his uniform. She imagined him walking the railroad tracks, slightly buzzed, near cars loaded with tons of coal or operating industrial ovens with temperatures hovering around 2,000 degrees.

A few years ago, she interviewed other men who worked at the coke plant in preparation for a potential oral history project for which her father refused to be interviewed. He was aggravated by her curiosity about the past, but the other men and their families shared her nostalgia. The men were always surprised to learn she was Billy's daughter. "You're crazy Bill's daughter?" one of them asked, astonished. She interviewed an elderly couple at their home, Ron and Eileen. Ron was in his eighties and connected to an oxygen tank. He walked around his house, holding the long tubes so as not to trip, looking for items to show her—his electronic time card, photographs, a tumbler he had received from the company as a retirement gift. His wife laughed as she told the story of how she used to wash Ron's uniforms until OSHA figured out the suits were covered with toxic dust. Some of the men her father worked with died of cancer or suffered from respiratory problems, but somehow Billy had been spared. As a hobby, Ron kept track of the plant's history. He showed Amy a list of every person who had worked there. She found her father's name: Billy Pritchett. Start Date: 1965.

When she was in graduate school she took a class in Appalachian Studies, but felt somewhat at odds with the idealized version of rural family life other students seemed to be mourning. Her father had worked around coal over forty years, but he hadn't been a miner and he wasn't a family man. On both sides of Amy's family, small farms had been abandoned for more profitable and secure jobs at the factories in town. Hardly anyone in Amy's family even owned a home. There was no *homeplace* other than a small farm run by an eccentric unmarried brother and sister, John and Helen Callahan, her maternal grandmother's siblings. Uncle John and Aunt Helen had lived all their lives in the farmhouse where they were born. The house had only basic electricity, a few dangling bare light bulbs and no running water or indoor plumbing. The only heat was from two potbellied stoves in the downstairs rooms and the coal stove in the kitchen. The house was built in the late 1800s and was probably grand at one time, but by the 1970s it was gray from lack of paint and so old it leaned forward as if it might collapse at any second. Uncle John had retired from the steel mill and had two grown sons from different women, neither of whom he had bothered to marry, but he continued to live at the house with his sister until he died when Amy was twelve. Aunt Helen died two months later. The family liked to gossip about how Uncle John, "the old codger," who had lived through the Great Depression and didn't trust banks, kept all his money in a brown paper sack under his big feather bed. *How much do you think is under there? Ten thousand? Fifty thousand? I bet he has a hundred thousand dollars under that bed!* After he died his sons ransacked the house and found the notorious paper sack with thirty thousand dollars inside. Uncle John had inherited the farm from his father. Aunt Helen being a mere daughter inherited nothing. The farm was eventually sold off in small parcels to people who put trailer homes on it.

 Once or twice a month Barb took Amy and Maryanne to eat Sunday dinner at the old house. Aunt Helen cooked the large meal on a coal stove. There was always fried chicken, corn bread, fresh vegetables from the garden, or from the jars Helen canned every year. There was a formal dining room with heavy furniture and a glass cabinet that contained the family china, but they always ate in the kitchen on everyday plates, next to the stove where it was warm. Amy and Maryanne liked to pump water from the well out back or pick vegetables from the large garden. They were warned not to go near the deep well in the front yard and to watch out for snakes. If they had to go to the bathroom there was an outhouse. The privy had two holes cut side by side. Amy and Maryanne found this hilarious. After dinner Aunt Helen liked to put the girls to work shucking corn or stringing green beans on the front porch, while the adults sat in big wooden rockers and chatted in the parlor. Amy and Maryanne ran in the garden and poked around in the barns, imagining the livestock that used to live there. Amy could remember when Helen and John kept horses, but now the barns were empty except for some old farm equipment.

A few times a year Aunt Helen insisted Amy and Maryanne come into her freezing cold sewing room and undress and be measured for the Easter dresses and unstylish school clothes she made for them every year—polyester pants with elastic waistlines and matching vests. Amy found scraps of these same materials sewn into crazy quilts Aunt Helen gave to them at Christmas. She took one of the quilts to college. Looking at the quilt years later brought back memories of those Sunday afternoons, shivering in her underwear, while Aunt Helen measured her bust, hips and waist with her cold, bony hands. The old woman always smelled like she had just been tending a fire. At the end of these visits Aunt Helen, who was frail and bent over from old age, would go outside and open the heavy doors to the cellar and descend down the narrow stone stairs into darkness. A few minutes later she would emerge with jars of jams and vegetables clanking in her apron. In the summer they would go home with bags of fresh vegetables. Because Barb was Aunt's Helen's favorite niece, she always slipped her some money before they left.

Those Sunday afternoons were an adventure. Aside from these visits, their lives were lived out of sync with nature—in apartment complexes, driving in cars amid coal dust and fumes from the factories. The sounds of trains and rumbling coal trucks and factory whistles signaling shift changes were more familiar to her than a rushing creek or a clucking chicken.

One day Amy called Billy and he casually announced the company had finally demolished the coke plant. Some of his buddies and neighbors at the motel where he lived had watched from across the road. Amy was so stunned she burst into tears. She found a video of the demolition on YouTube. The plant had been in the town for over one hundred years. Forty-one of those her father had worked there. In less than ten seconds it was gone. How did he feel about that?

"Why you so interested in it?" he asked. As usual he was irritated by her questions.

She never imagined the plant wouldn't be there or that her mother would move away before Amy had the chance to make sense of it all; or that, in the end, her only connection to Big Sandy would be Billy. When she finally had the chance to visit, Amy drove immediately through town, down I-23 towards Catlettsburg, and stood next to the railroad tracks that had run alongside the plant. She saw for herself the now vacant and toxic land. Like any death the finality was difficult to comprehend.

Made in the USA
Middletown, DE
09 April 2017